MICROSAURS

TINY-RAPTOR PACK ATTACK

MICROSAURS

TINY-RAPTOR PACK ATTACK

DUSTIN HANSEN

Feiwel and Friends
New York

A FEIWEL AND FRIENDS BOOK
An imprint of Macmillan Publishing Group, LLC

Our books may be purchased in bulk for promotional, educational, or business use. Please contact your local bookseller or the Macmillan Corporate and Premium Sales Department at (800) 221-7945 ext. 5442 or by e-mail at MacmillanSpecialMarkets@macmillan.com.

Library of Congress Cataloging-in-Publication Data
Names: Hansen, Dustin, author, illustrator.
Title: Microsaurs: tiny-raptor pack attack / Dustin Hansen.
Description: First edition. | New York: Feiwel and Friends, 2017. | Series: Microsaurs ; 2 | Summary: Professor Penrod sends Danny and Lin a mysterious package filled with biting, scratching microsaurs hungry enough to chew through walls, along with a very large microsaur egg. | Description based on print version record and CIP data provided by publisher; resource not viewed.
Identifiers: LCCN 2016037931 (print) | LCCN 2017017612 (ebook) | ISBN 9781250090270 (ebook) | ISBN 9781250090256 (hardcover) | ISBN 9781250090263 (paperback)
Subjects: | CYAC: Dinosaurs—Fiction. | Size—Fiction. | Friendship—Fiction. | Inventions—Fiction. | Adventure and adventurers—Fiction. | BISAC: JUVENILE FICTION / Animals / Dinosaurs & Prehistoric Creatures. | JUVENILE FICTION / Animals / Pets.
Classification: LCC PZ7.1.H3643 (ebook) | LCC PZ7.1.H3643 Tin 2017 (print) | DDC [Fic]—dc23
LC record available at https://lccn.loc.gov/2016037931

Book design by Liz Dresner
Feiwel and Friends logo designed by Filomena Tuosto

First Edition—2017

10 9 8 7 6 5 4 3 2 1

mackids.com

For Malorie, who shares my favorite Bs:
Broadway, board games, and, of course, books.

CHAPTER 1
THE BOLT!

"This is the last lap, Danny. We've got to catch up!" Lin shouted as she gripped the controller for *The Bolt*, our remote control car, in her hands. The little dune buggy launched off the Spin Cycle, a jump made out of an old washing machine in the middle of the world's greatest dirt racing track.

"Wings engaged!" I pressed a button on the screen of my dad's old smartphone. I had updated his SpyZoom app to operate the upgrades for *The Bolt*, our jet-fueled,

electric-blue, highly modified, nitro-equipped, twelve-inch-long, remote control racer. We were in second place, but I could almost smell the victory, we were so close. Or maybe it was just the jet fuel.

A year ago some kids started racing RC cars in an abandoned dump, and it had really caught on. There wasn't a prize or a trophy for the winner, but there were bragging rights, and for Lin and me, that was more than enough.

"How close are we to that orange hunk of junk?" Lin asked. She slammed on the brake button and *The Bolt* drifted around an old toilet bowl, half buried in the dirt.

We didn't mess around with the normal races; we were in the Super Modified Team Class. A two-person race with one driver and one copilot. But the best thing about the modified team race was that you could upgrade your RC car in any way you could imagine. No rules. No regrets.

I checked my phone. A video streamed from a camera no bigger than an un-popped kernel of popcorn glued to the top of *The Bolt*. I had a perfect view of everything in front of our RC car. An orange truck with a homemade yellow flame job painted on the side filled the screen. It was twice as big as our car, spit glops of mud from its toothy tires, and it had a jar full of dangerous-looking green sludge bouncing around in its truck bed.

"I think we can catch him if we use Sonic-Earth Shake to boost us down the slide," I said.

"All right. Bring on the noise," Lin said.

Lin swerved around a bald tractor tire, then shot *The Bolt* over an old mattress. She aimed the nose of our car directly at a rusted-out slide that had once been the biggest thing in the Jefferson Elementary playground. *The Bolt* burst up the old slide, but before it reached the top a beetle-shaped car with eyelashes over its headlights blinked past us so fast it looked like a streak of sparkly purple fingernail polish.

"What was that?" Lin asked as the purple blur whizzed by and caught up to the orange truck.

"Do it again, Daddy!" said a high-pitched voice that we both recognized at once. "I'm winning, Daddy! Do it again!"

"Oh great, it's Icky Vicky," Lin said just loud enough for me to hear.

Somehow we hadn't noticed her standing in the drivers' area before the race started, but I glanced to my left and sure enough, it was her. Victoria Van-Varbles, the daughter of the mayor, Valerie Van-Varbles, and the richest kid in the entire county. Probably the entire STATE!

It wasn't the first time I'd seen Vicky and her purple glitter-mobile at the races, but last time she couldn't drive the car in a straight line, let alone pass Lin and me on the final lap. But one glance and it all made sense. She wasn't driving the car at all. A guy dressed in a leather jacket covered in brightly colored logos was driving the car for her, and her dad

was copiloting, working a large panel of trigger buttons to launch her store-bought, overpriced upgrades.

"She's not even driving," I said to Lin, but Lin didn't care about that right then. She was too busy trying to win!

"Fire the Grappling-Grabber!" Lin said.

I tapped the grappling hook icon on my SpyZoom app and crosshairs raised up in front of the camera. I used the smartphone to line up a perfect shot, right at the back of Vicky's purple RC car. "FIRE AWAY!" I shouted, then slammed a finger down on the launch button.

A small hook shot out of the side cannon glued to *The Bolt*. The hook buzzed through the air, then wrapped around the back bumper of Victoria Van-Varbles's sparkly purple car.

"Direct hit! Crank it in," Lin shouted. I swiped a command on my phone and a little motor inside *The Bolt* began to wind the dental floss back up onto the spool.

"Daddy, they are cheating! Do something," Vicky said in a voice so high-pitched I thought it might crack the plastic windshield on *The Bolt*.

"Oh, I don't think you can cheat in the Super Modified Team Class, darling. That is what makes it fun," Vicky's dad said, but that just made her mad.

"It's not fun for *me*! Do something or I will!" Vicky said. She stomped her foot so hard I thought I felt the ground shake.

With the help of the hook, we quickly slipped right up behind Vicky's car and the orange truck. The grappling hook was working perfectly, but I had one more trick to try and just enough time before we crossed the finish line.

"Ready for the Hammer of Doom?" I asked Lin.

"Oh yeah, bring it down HARD!"

"They have a doom hammer thingy, Daddy!" Vicky jumped up and down, and her black braids bounced higher with every shout.

"Push a button or something! LIGHT THEM ON FIRE!" Vicky screamed.

"Get as close as you can," I said to Lin. She bumped into the back of Vicky's car, and it swerved over and buzzed against the wheels of the huge orange truck.

"Close enough?" she asked. But instead of answering I discharged the Hammer of Doom. The top of *The Bolt* split in two, and a big red hammer extended out. It was cocked back on a spring I had taken out of an old mini-trampoline. A second before it smashed down on Vicky's car and the big orange truck, Vicky's expert driver swerved and smashed into the orange truck. The Hammer of Doom missed them both, clobbering down in front of us, creating nothing more than a big splat of mud.

The jar of green goop in the back of the orange truck teetered and bobbled. Vicky's dad grinned and pushed a button on his controller.

A poof of shiny purple glitter exploded from the rear of Vicky's car just as the green goop

tumbled from the back of the truck, and all I could see was green slime and purple sparkles. The camera was no use now.

With its engine full of glittery goop, *The Bolt* sputtered to a stop. The orange truck did about twelve somersaults, and then its race came to an end in a cloud of dust. But that wasn't the worst part. Not by far.

"I won, I won! Did you see that, everyone? I totally won that race!" Victoria Van-Varbles shouted at the top of her voice, scaring every bird, squirrel, and human within ten miles.

Lin growled like a bear that had just lost its honey pot to a clever chipmunk. A bright purple, hair-bow-wearing, totally-annoying chipmunk.

Vicky spoke as she walked away. "It was fun winning, Daddy. But I want a grappling hook and a big hammer thingy on my car for next week. Oh, and a bottle of green goop, too. I'm never going to lose again!"

Lin grumbled, and I could tell that she'd had enough of Icky Vicky. I tried to grab Lin's shirt to hold her back, but I missed and she took off after Vicky.

"Oh yeah?" Lin asked. "You're never going to lose again? Want to make a bet?"

Vicky turned around and gave Lin a smile so sweet that I think I got a cavity by just looking at her. "Oh hi, Lin. I didn't see you there," she said, which was totally a lie. "Um, sorry. I don't bet."

"Well, that's too bad because I'd bet *The Bolt* and all its upgrades, plus half a box of chocolate-covered raisins that you can't beat me again right now," Lin said.

"Oh, I don't want that trashed-up car. Besides, I already beat you. Why would I want to do it again?" Vicky said.

"Come on, honey," her dad said, putting his arm on her shoulder. "You've got ballet in fifteen minutes. We don't want to be late."

"It won't take me fifteen minutes to beat you," Lin said. "Or maybe you're just scared."

Victoria Van-Varbles put her hands on her hips and cocked her head to the left. The sickly sweet look on her face swapped to serious in a flash. "Check my schedule, Daddy. I need fifteen minutes to teach Miss Lin Song a lesson."

"Let's just wait until next week, Victoria, darling," her dad said.

"Um, no. I need to beat her as soon as possible. I'm not scared of anything," Vicky said. "Let's do it today."

Vicky's father didn't argue, and I could tell she was very used to getting her way. "Oh, all right, sweetheart. Hang on." Vicky's dad pulled a tablet out of his jacket pocket and started scrolling through her calendar. "Ballet at eleven. Lunch at your mom's office today at twelve thirty. Then there's soccer practice, yoga, and swimming lessons. You're booked until four thirty today, Victoria, darling."

"Lemme check my schedule," Lin said. She pulled an imaginary calendar out of her back pocket, licked her finger, then started turning through the pages. "Nothing. Watch some TV. Corn dogs for lunch. Oh, look at that. Four thirty—Beat Vicky at the Dump Track. You're already in my schedule."

"Better make it four forty-five. I'll need to

blow-dry my hair after swimming. I want to look good for my championship selfie at five," Vicky said. She turned and started walking away with her dad and the professional driver. She stopped and looked over her shoulder. "Oh, and on second thought, I do want that car of yours. Even if it is a hunk of junk, it will look nice on my trophy shelf." She waved, gave that sugary smile to Lin and me again, then skipped away with her pom-pom braids bouncing around her shoulders.

"She's going down," Lin said quietly to me.

"Like an old tree in a hurricane," I agreed.

CHAPTER 2
SPRING CLEANING—LITERALLY

If your RC car is full of glitter and boogery slime, my house is probably the best place in our entire town to clean it up. Maybe even in the whole wide world.

My dad is an inventor for SpyZoom Technologies, and he works out of his home lab. He has everything from micro-welders to toxic

cleaners in big blue barrels. He's got high-speed testing cameras, lasers, microscopes, computers, and so many tools he needs an entire wall of toolboxes to hold them all. The lab is even equipped with a stereo system, a mini-fridge, a toaster oven that makes some pretty great crispy burritos, and a microwave for pizza and corn dogs.

In fact, next to the Microterium, Professor Penrod's top secret barn packed with Microsaurs, it is probably my favorite place on earth.

Parts from *The Bolt* were spread out on the workbench, a neat stack of cleaned parts on the left, and a pile of mucky-mess on the right. Lin and I had cleaned all *The Bolt*'s upgrades, and we were testing to make sure they were in working order before putting them back on.

"You know how to put this all together again, right?" Lin asked.

I looked at her over the magnifying glass I'd

been peering through while working on a release
spring. "You know who you're talking to, don't
ya?" I said.

"Yeah, yeah. I know, but that's a lot of parts. Even for you, Danny," she said. She put down the cotton swabs. She was done with the whole cleaning thing. "Hey. What is there to eat around here? I'm starving."

"The fridge is full of good stuff. Want to heat up some pizza? There's corn dogs in there, too," I said.

"Sure. Can I use the Bunsen burner to toast the pizza again?" Lin asked as she skipped over to the mini-fridge.

"No. My dad said he cleaned mozzarella out of there for a week. Just nuke it in the microwave," I said. I snapped the release spring onto the lever arm of the Slap-Clapper, tapped the button on my SpyZoom app to test it, and it smacked the table so hard it made a loud WHACK! "Well, they all still work. That purple bug is going to get squashed."

Lin was crouched down, looking into the fridge. "Where's your dad today?"

"He's testing his new Whiff-O-Zapper device in the field. He said he'd be back before dinner," I said as my phone started to buzz. "Hey. Maybe that's him." I de-gunked my hands on my shirt, then tapped a button to answer the phone and the screen filled with green grass and sunshine.

"Hey, Dad. Is that you?" I asked as Lin started piling frozen pizza and corn dogs on the workbench next to the RC car parts.

The grass started to rustle, then a man wearing a camouflage hat covered in ferns and weeds popped up from the grass. His face was

streaked with mud, and there were sticks woven
into his thick mustache.

"It's me, Penrod!" the grass-covered man said.

Lin leaned in to see the phone screen. "Hey!
How you been, Penny, old pal?"

"Prodigious. Perky! PERFECT, Lin, my young pal! And how have you two been lately?"

"We're doing great. We've been checking in on the Microterium like you asked before you left for China," I said. "Bruno is getting so big you won't recognize him."

Lin and I went to the Microterium two, sometimes three times a day. We couldn't get enough of the place! We discovered the professor's secret lab by following a GPS-stealing tiny-dactyl who led us on an adventure that ruined my favorite shirt, tested my fear of heights, and taught us that riding a Microsaur sure beats walking.

"And I've been teaching Zip-Zap how to do flips. He's really good at it, too," Lin said.

"With or without you on his back at the time?" Professor Penrod asked.

"With, of course. You'll totally have to

try it out. It makes your tummy go all swishy. I love it SO MUCH I can't hardly stand it."

"Oh, that's wonderful. I knew the Microsaurs would be in good hands with you two," Penrod said.

"How are things in China, Professor?" I asked.

"Well, funny you should ask. The food has been amazing, the people are super nice, but the satellite cell phone connection out here is horrible. So I better get down to business. I need to tell you that I've sent a very special package to the Microterium. It should be there now! It's very important that you rush over and let the contents out immediately. Give them a little room to run, because after sitting in a crate for a couple of weeks, I'm sure they'll need it," he said.

I was so excited I wanted to sprint to the Microterium right away.

"So, what's inside this package?" Lin asked as

she stuffed frozen pizza and corn dogs into my backpack. I guess she was ready to go, too.

"Oh, you won't believe it . . ." Penrod said.

". . . a pack of . . ." The video skipped for a moment and the audio fuzzed out.

"Uh-oh. I think we're losing him," Lin said.

"And there's a secret compartment . . ." Penrod said. "And a wire mesh wall to keep them . . ." Another fuzz out. Another jumpy video screen.

"Penny! Can you hear us?" Lin said. She tapped the screen of my phone with a frozen corn dog.

"I don't think hitting the phone with an ice-dog is going to improve his cell connection in China," I said.

"It might," she said as she thunked it again. Penrod's face started moving instantly.

"I hope the wall will hold. I'm pretty sure it will, but you've got to hurry. Oh, and be careful, you might want to bring a . . ." Penrod said, just before the screen froze one last time, then it went black.

"The power of corn dogs!" Lin said. She reached over me to try to whack my phone with the corn dog one more time. I pulled it away before she could crack the screen.

"What do you think he was going to say? Bring a what?"

"I'm sure we'll be fine. The important part is that we get to the Microterium fast. You ready?" I took the last frozen corn dog from Lin's hand, slipped it in my backpack, then started stuffing *The Bolt*'s upgrade parts into the pack as well.

"I'm ready, but why are you bringing all that stuff?" Lin asked.

"Well, you never know when a Sonic-Earth Shaker, a Goo-Cannon, Grappling-Grabber, a Hammer of Doom, or a Slap-Clapper will come in handy. Race you to the Microterium," I said. I zipped up my backpack and we took off running.

CHAPTER 3
BACK IN THE MICROTERIUM

It's a good thing we met Professor Penrod when we did, because he needed our help. His trip to China would have been impossible without us to stay behind and keep things in the Microterium running smoothly. And not just that—Lin and I are expert secret keepers, too, which comes in handy, because the Microterium is super top secret.

At first when I saw Professor Penrod's house, it totally gave me the creeps. I actually thought it was a haunted mansion. His house is tucked away in the woods, surrounded by a tall iron gate and overgrown weeds, and snarling dinosaur gargoyles stare down at you from the corners of his roof to finish off the mood. But it didn't worry me anymore. We'd been back every day since we first discovered the Microterium, and now when I saw the house I got all excited, because I knew there were adventures behind that iron gate.

Lin and I slipped between the bars and walked through the weeds behind the spooky old house, toward a rickety old barn.

The Microterium was hidden behind a fake wall inside the barn. Professor Penrod had built the space to keep the Microsaurs he'd rescued safe, happy, and healthy. Oh, and to keep them super top secret. There were more than one hundred of the little dinosaurs living and playing inside the secret jungle hideout, and there was easily room for a thousand more. It really was a Microsaur paradise.

We made our way to the old barn and let ourselves in. The door to the Microterium creaked on its rusty hinges. It took a couple of seconds for my eyes to adjust to the dark as we stepped inside. I looked around for a while, then spotted Professor Penrod's package, right there in the middle of the floor. It was no bigger than one of Lin's little sister's bunny slippers. It was covered in bright red stamps and all kinds of writing and marks that I couldn't read.

"There it is," I said to Lin, and we knelt down for a closer look.

"It's not very big. I was hoping for something huge! Something really growly and awesome," Lin said.

"Those are airholes punched in the top," I said.

"Yeah, and check out the label," Lin said.

A bright yellow sticker was stretched across the top of the box. On it were printed a few, not-so-comforting words:

⚠ CAUTION

Contents may bite.

HARD

"Oh man. I wonder what's inside," I said. I leaned closer. I could hear a tiny scratching, clicking noise that totally gave me the willies. The noise was coming from a spot in the front of the package, where the little creatures had almost chomped through. "They're trying to bite their way out."

Lin jumped up and sprang to the back wall. Professor Penrod was pretty careful about keeping the Microterium secret. The room we were in was a cross between a barn and a science lab, but if you twisted a framed picture of his favorite childhood dog, Bruno, who was dressed as a clown in the photo, the back wall would lower, opening up to the massive Microterium. Lin gave the photo a twist.

"I can't believe he sent us a box full of toothy, scratchy Microsaurs. That is so AWESOME!" she said as the wall started to move.

"Yeah, if you love microsized prehistoric beasts with teeth that chew through walls, then it is really awesome," I said and even while I said it I could feel electric shivers buzzing up my spine.

"I know, RIGHT!?" Lin said. "It's exactly what the Microterium needs. CHOMPERS!"

"Actually, I'm more of a 'eats grass and stomps in mud puddles' kind of guy," I said.

"Come on, Danny. Let's shrink and get a better look," Lin said. She was standing on a metal step beneath one of Professor Penrod's fantastic inventions, the Shrink-A-Fier. It was built right into the Microterium. Copper tubing wound around to cool the liquid boiling in a glass bulb the shape and size of a pumpkin, and a nozzle that looked like a big shiny showerhead gleamed in the sunshine that came in through the roof of the Microterium.

"Um, I'm thinking I'd rather meet these guys for the first time when I'm eighty times their size," I said.

"No way. NO WAY! Dude. We've got to see them eye to eye. You know what they say: You only have one chance to make a first impression," Lin said. She was bouncing up and down on the metal step, which also happened to be the trigger that started up the Shrink-A-Fier. A motor whirled overhead, and the shrinking liquid started to flow into the copper pipes.

"Yeah, I was just hoping that the first impression I made on these guys was less bite-sized," I said nervously.

I scooped up the package and placed it right next to the Shrink-A-Fier. Then I unloaded

The Bolt and the upgrade parts and stacked them neatly next to the package of Microsaurs. I cleared my throat, stood up straight and brave, then I joined Lin on the metal step.

"Why did you do that?" Lin asked.

"The parts are heavy, and besides, I wanted to get a close-up look at *The Bolt*'s engine after we are Shrink-A-Fied. It's running pretty good, but I think I might be able to tweak a bit more power out of it," I said.

Lin snapped her helmet strap under her chin as she prepared for an adventure. "I'm good with more power," she said, then gave me a wink. "I love the Shrink-A-Fier. It always makes me feel like a snowflake. You ready?"

"No. Not really," I said, but it was too late. The shrinking had already begun.

I looked up at the Mini-Maxitron Reduction Nozzle, which Lin had renamed the Shrinker-Sprinkler. I blinked as it puffed out a small spray of frozen CRPs, Carbonic Reduction Particles. The first time the shrinking process happened, I was pretty freaked out. But after Professor Penrod explained how the technology worked, and I had a couple of chances to get used to it, I actually started to enjoy the whole process.

The CRPs danced around us, and all of a sudden I had a familiar shoved-in-a-freezer-full-of-glitter feeling, and my tummy rolled with excitement. Lin's eyes were closed and she was smiling while hugging her skateboard. For a moment I almost thought I was falling, then the two of us shrank to the size of tiny, dried-up raisins. But without the wrinkles, of course.

I was still dizzy from the speedy shrinking

when I heard Lin jump onto her skateboard. She was speeding toward the little package Professor Penrod sent us, only now it was as big as a house.

"Told ya, Danny. It's snowflakey, isn't it?" Lin yelled over her shoulder. "Last one there's a rotten egg."

I started running, even though I knew the rotten egg thing wasn't true. Lin pretty much said it every time we raced, and if it were true, I'd be the rottenest egg ever in the history of rotten eggs.

By the time I arrived at the box, Lin was already looking for a way in. The faint scratching and clicking noise I'd heard when I was regular-sized was as loud as a thunderstorm now that we were tiny. Lin stood on the other side of the scratching, hammering against the box with her skateboard.

"What are you doing?" I asked. My heart

was beating so fast I felt like I'd just climbed a thousand stairs, but it wasn't just from the running.

"I'm letting them run free." Lin gave up on using her skateboard. "Hold on, little toothy guys. I'll find another way in," Lin said, then she ran around to the back of the box.

"Umm, maybe keeping them in the box is a better idea," I said.

"But Professor Penrod said we should let them out. Remember?"

"Yeah, sure I remember, but I'm not sure we got all the information. Maybe we should call him," I said, trying to be more logical than brave, which is another way of saying I was a little bit scared.

"Hey, Danny. Come help. I found the way in," Lin said, then I heard a little *RIIIIIP!*

I found Lin on the other side of the box, holding a piece of tape as wide as a sleeping bag in her hands. She smiled at me and gave the tape another tug. *RIIIIIP!*

"It's a door, Danny. Penrod thought of everything," she said.

I took a deep breath, then let it out in one big huff. "Okay, but let me just say, for the record, that I think we should—"

RIIIIP!

"Less talking and more pulling, Danny. What are you worried about? Do you think Professor Penrod would do something that would put us in danger?"

"I think his sense of what is dangerous is as murky as yours. Especially when it comes to Microsaurs. Do I need to remind you that he let us fly in a bottle-cap basket tied to a pterodactyl?" I said.

"You can remind me all you want, as long as you help"—Lin yanked on the tape and it tore a small hole in the box—"me." She yanked again and the box split a bit more. "PULL!" She yanked the tape one more time. I could see it was going to be impossible for her to do alone, and we did promise Penrod that we would help.

Whatever was inside had to come out. Sure, the box was filled with airholes, but I didn't know if there was food and fresh water inside the package.

"All right, all right. But if I become a Microsaur's lunch, I'm leaving my comic book collection to Stanley Hobbs," I said. Lin dropped the tape and looked at me, wrinkled her eyebrows, and put her hands on her hips.

"Are you kidding me? Stanley Hobbs? He doesn't even *like* comics. Why would you say that?" Lin said.

"Better not let me become lunch," I said. I grabbed the tape, then leaned back and put my weight against it. One of the scratching things inside poked its beak through the little hole and even though I was still scared, I was the tiniest bit excited to see what was inside the package. "You going to help me or what?"

Lin rolled her eyes at me. She grabbed ahold

of the tape, then started counting. "3 . . . 2 . . . 1 . . . PULL!" she said, and we both yanked as hard as we could.

The tape gave way and we fell on our backs, thumping down to the hardwood floor and stripping the tape clean off. The door flap fell away, and the scratching from inside the box stopped as Lin and I waited, holding our breath to see what Penrod had sent us from halfway around the world.

Lin couldn't wait any longer, so she jumped up and called to the new visitors. "Here, toothy-toothy," Lin said.

"Do you have to call them that?" I shout-whispered.

"Come on out, scratchy-scratchy," Lin said. She turned her head and looked at me with a smile. "Is that better?"

"Yeah. Much better, thanks," I said as I dusted off my pants.

Lin took a few steps back and stood right by my side, then she flung her arms out wide like she wanted to hug every creature in the box.

"Welcome to the Microterium!" Lin shouted.

For a second nothing happened, then a pack of feathers, beaks, and scaly legs exploded from the box. They squawked and clicked their way across the hardwood floor. Then they *eeeped* and shrieked as they surrounded Lin and me. Maybe I panicked, or maybe I really was getting more brave. I jumped in front of Lin, then held out my hands, backing down a half circle of hungry-looking Microsaurs.

"You calm down right now!" I shouted in my most heroic voice. It surprised me, and probably Lin, too, but most of all it got the toothy pack of Microsaurs' attention. They stopped making their clicking noises and tilted their heads and stared at me.

Controlling a pack of tiny-raptors felt pretty amazing, but I could tell it wouldn't last long.

"Now what do we do?" I asked Lin.

Lin unzipped my backpack, stuffed her hand inside, and pulled out the answer to my question. She held a corn dog and a slice of frozen pizza over her head.

"Hey, you toothy little guys! I'll bet you've never had

pepperoni. Have you?" The raptors' glares shifted to Lin, then they all started sniffing the air. "And I KNOW you've never had a corn dog."

"I think it's working," I said. The biggest of the raptors stuck out a blue tongue and licked his beak, then raised his nose in the air.

"Walk with me, Danny," Lin said. We backed away slowly. We headed backward, off the hardwood floor and onto the metal step. The pack of tiny-raptors moved with us. They were getting closer and closer. So close I could smell their breath, which wasn't the best experience I'd ever had in the Microterium.

Focused on Lin and her frozen treats, the pack of Microsaurs forgot all about me. They kept bumping into me, and I was starting to freak out a little. "Lin, ummm, you need to do something pretty soon. They are looking pretty hungry."

"I know they are," Lin said in the same voice she used to talk to her dog, Mr. Bones. "Who's a hungry little toothy-woothy? Are you hungry, wittle puppy-saurus?" One of them took a snap at the pizza in her right hand. The sound made me jump, and I felt like running in any direction that didn't include pizza, corn dogs, or a pack of hungry raptors.

"How about you, little scratchy-clawsey? You want a bite?" Lin asked the big, blue-tongued raptor. He jumped and nearly yanked the corn dog out of Lin's hand, but she pulled it away just in time.

As Lin and I walked onto the step with the hungry bunch, the sound of their sharp claws scratching against the metal step was enough to make my hair stand at attention. Then just before we fell off the edge, Lin stopped.

"Fetch!" she yelled. She chucked the pizza and corn dog as far as she could. The pack of tiny-raptors half flew, half fell over the edge, chasing the frozen snacks and entering the sunshiny Microterium.

I looked over the edge, trying to take deep breaths to calm my beating heart. The raptors landed safely on the ground and began fighting

over the snacks and exploring their new home.

"Well. That worked better than I expected," Lin said.

"Really? What did you expect?" I said as I stood and joined her by the package.

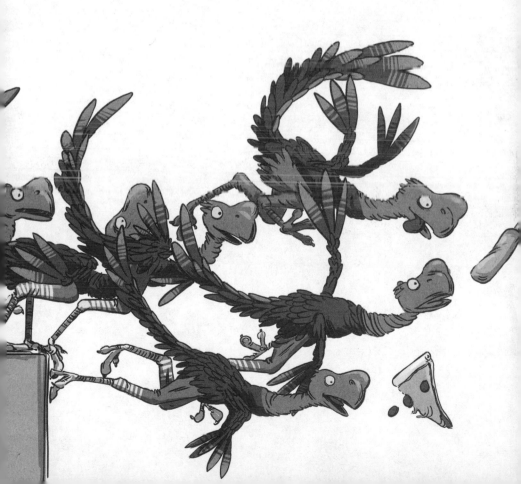

"I expected Stanley Hobbs would be getting a new comic book collection by now," Lin said with a big grin on her face.

I smiled back, glad to be rid of the pack of feathers, claws, and chompers. "Come on. Let's go see what else is inside this box."

CHAPTER 5
INSIDE THE BOX

"How many flashlights do you have with you, Danny?" Lin asked as we entered the package.

"Three," I said. "No wait, four." I fished two out of my pack. I passed the biggest one to Lin.

"Thanks," she said. We took a few more steps inside the dark package, then clicked on

our lights. It seemed larger on the inside as we waded through shredded paper all around that came up to our knees.

"What's all this stuff?" Lin asked.

"I think it's like packing peanuts, but for Microsaurs. You know, stuff to keep them comfy as they made their way halfway around the world," I said. I swung my flashlight to the back wall. There were two pouches taped to the wall; one had a few drops of water left in it, and the other was about half full of something that looked like runny mashed potatoes. The metal tubes that hung down from the pouches were dented with tooth marks.

"Whoa. Those things really do bite HARD! The sticker on the box was not kidding around," Lin said. "I'm impressed." I shined my flashlight on her face and the strange lighting made her look a little crazy as she grinned down at the bite marks.

"Impressed isn't the first word that came to my mind. Worried? Nervous? Terrified? Yeah, that's it. Teeth that can dent metal pipes. Yup, that's terrifying," I said.

"They're harmless, Danny. Totally, one hundred percent harmless. Unless you smell like pizza and corn dogs. Then you better worry," Lin said as she turned and kept exploring the dark package.

"You know that is *exactly* how I smell right now, don't you?" I said.

"Hey! Look at this!" Lin said, changing the topic, which was totally, one hundred percent fine with me.

Her flashlight beam reflected off a metal grate stapled into the back of the package. I added my flashlight beam to hers and for a moment, I forgot how to blink. Forgot how to breathe. Heck, I forgot how to forget.

"That's the mesh wall Professor Penrod was talking about," I said.

"Yeah, and they almost got through it," Lin said.

The wire mesh that separated the raptors from whatever was behind it was woven together so thick that we couldn't see through it. The raptors had twisted, yanked, and fought

against the mesh, making it look like iron spaghetti, but the wall looked strong. Too strong for us to cut through even if we were regular-sized.

"They wanted in pretty bad," I said.

"Yeah. It's probably full of rare Chinese corn dogs," Lin said.

A thought popped into my head that I didn't want to share, but my mouth started talking before I could stop it. "Or maybe the raptors didn't twist up this metal wall at all. Maybe the raptors were trying to get out before whatever is behind this mesh got out and ate them," I said, slowly backing away.

"Oh . . . MY . . . GOSH! You might be right! What could scare away a pack of tiny-raptors?" Lin grabbed the wall and started shaking it.

She shook the bars until she realized it wouldn't budge. She slumped to the floor, nearly burying herself up to her neck in torn paper shreds.

"It's no use. We'll have to go to the Fruity Stars Lab, use the Expand-O-Matic, and come back and open it as big guys," she said. "That's a lot of walking."

"Well, there might be another way," I said, my mouth working faster than my brain again.

Lin's face brightened, and she smiled up at me. "Lay it on me, science boy. Are we going to math our way in?"

"No. Even better. We're going to use the Hammer of Doom," I said.

CHAPTER 6
THE HAMMER OF DOOM

When I was building the upgrade parts for *The Bolt*, I tried to think of everything. I made the parts out of lightweight plastic and titanium scraps I found in my dad's lab. But I guess I didn't think I'd be trying to use the Hammer of Doom to tear down a metal wall while I was the size of a housefly. Moving the huge hammer wasn't easy, but after a lot of grunting and groaning, we were finally able to get it into place.

"Do you think this will work?" Lin asked.

"That mesh wall is DOOMED!" I said.

I launched the SpyZoom app, then pushed a blinking red button to fire my secret weapon. The Hammer of Doom sprang into action, coming down with a powerful *THUD* as it tore through the metal mesh wall.

Lin jumped and shouted, pumped her arms,

danced like a robot, then ran over to me and gave me a high five so hard that my hand went numb. "That was SO AMAZING!"

I knew I was smiling, but I couldn't help it. The hammer ripping through a wall was totally satisfying. Little shreds of paper floated down all around us. "Yeah, that was pretty sweet."

"Come on. Let's go take a look," Lin said.

"If we have to," I said, still not sure that I wanted to come face-to-face with something that required a metal fence.

Lin bounced over to the new opening in the mesh wall, hurdled over the Hammer of Doom, and disappeared into the dark of the box.

"Danny. You have got to come and see this. And don't worry. It won't bite. In fact, it's totally toothless."

I leaned into the hole in the wall and looked around. Light poured in through an airhole, shining a perfect spotlight on Lin and the largest egg I'd ever seen in my life.

"Whoa. That is ginormous," I said.

The egg rested in a hammock made from

yellow yarn, which was now the size of the
wide ropes you'd expect on a pirate ship. The
hammock held the egg nice and snug, protecting
it as it made the trip across the ocean without a
single crack. Lin climbed up the ropes and sat on
top of the egg like a helmet-wearing bird.

"What are you doing?" I asked.

"I'm going to hatch it," she said.

I laughed, but Lin looked 110 percent serious.

"That's an interesting idea, Lin, but we have to

get that thing to the Fruity Stars Lab as fast as we can."

Inside the Microterium, tucked away in a valley behind a big hill, Professor Penrod had built another lab inside an upside-down cereal box. It's where he kept his Expand-O-Matic and a few lab tools. Including a Bunsen burner that we could use to heat the place up nice and toasty. Lin had named the place the Fruity Stars Lab the minute she laid eyes on it and the name stuck.

"Why?" Lin asked. "It looks so comfy in its little yellow swing."

"For one thing, it's too cold. We need to get it to the Fruity Stars Lab to warm it up," I said.

"Why don't I just sit on it until it hatches? I mean, how warm is a bird's butt anyway?" Lin said as she started rubbing the eggshell with her hands and breathing on it with hot puffs of breath.

"Well, a bird can be pretty warm when it's covered in feathers, but that's not the only problem. Remember that pack of tiny-raptors that tried to chew their way into here? I'd say there is about a 94.7 percent chance they are heading back here right now," I said.

"Ooh, wait. Look. It has light blue specks on it! I love this egg more than anything in the world. I could hug it all day." She leaned against the egg, caressing it with her cheek and arms.

I couldn't help but laugh at Lin. For being such an adventure seeker, she sure was a hugger. Even if the thing she was hugging had a hard shell.

"Lin. Did you hear me? Those toothy Microsaurs are probably going to come back. And they might be coming back for the egg," I said.

Lin perked up so fast it was like she'd been poked with a pin. "They are NOT stealing my egg. EVER!"

"So, we have two choices. We hide it away in the Fruity Stars Lab, where we can get it nice and warm, or we hang around here and hope we have enough pizza and corn dogs to keep the pack of tiny-raptors happy," I said.

Lin slipped off the egg and stood right in front of me, a very serious look on her face. "They are not taking my egg. And they are not eating your pizza.

And they are NOT eating any more of my corn dogs. I have my limits, Danny," Lin said.

"All right. Then help me get this egg down. We're going to need your skateboard. I have an idea how we're going to get this little guy moving, but it won't be easy. I hope you enjoy pushing," I said.

"As much as you love to pull," Lin said, then spit on her hands, rubbed them together, and started untying the yarn hammock.

CHAPTER 7
HONK-HONK RETURNS!

It took a little planning and a whole lot of luck for us to lower the Microsaur egg off the metal step, but that is when the hard work really started.

"Oh my heck, this thing weighs a ton," Lin said as she pushed the egg with all her might.

The egg was still wrapped up in the yarn

hammock, and we used a few extra bits of rope to tie it to Lin's skateboard. The tiny wheels weren't all that helpful in the soft earth of the Microterium, but it was better than nothing.

"I don't think it's an actual ton, but if it were only one ounce in the real world, by the time we shrank down it would be about two hundred fifty pounds," I said as I tugged against the rope. "Well, that is unless you consider mass and density. I'll have to recalcu—"

"More pulley, less talky!" Lin cut me off as we came to another stop when the front wheels of the skateboard bumped into a rock.

"Right. Okay. 3 . . . 2 . . . 1 . . . HEAVE!" I said. Lin pushed and I pulled, but the egg didn't budge. We shoved and yanked until we were both red-faced-exhausted, then we slumped to the ground to catch our breath.

"There's got to be a better way," I said. I found the canteen in my backpack, took a big swig, then passed it to Lin.

"I'm all ears if you have an idea," Lin said, then she gulped about half the canteen down.

"What do you think is inside? It's pretty big for an egg," I said.

"I don't know, but I hope it's covered in scaly skin, with hooklike claws and more teeth than a gang of gators!" she said, acting out the creature she

imagined hiding inside the egg. The thought of finding a dangerous Microsaur inside the egg made Lin smile and her eyes sparkle.

"Or maybe it could be a friendly, puddle-stomping, broccoli-loving stegosaurus," I said.

"Ew!!! Broccoli! Gross, Danny. Why would you say something horrible like that?" Lin said, scrunching up her face and plugging her ears.

"Maybe it's another hadrosaur, like Honk-Honk," I said, then all at once, Lin and I had the same idea.

"Honk-Honk!" we both said at the same time.

"That's it. We need Honk-Honk," I said.

"She could easily carry the egg back to the Fruity Stars Lab for us," Lin said.

"Exactly! Now all we need is Professor Penrod's trumpet!" I said. Professor Penrod used a trumpet to call for his most helpful and loving Microsaur, Honk-Honk.

"We don't need a trumpet. I have an idea," Lin said.

A large vine grew at the base of a tree that dipped its roots into the creek. Halfway up the vine, orange, ice-cream-cone-shaped flowers bloomed. Lin climbed the vine, used both hands to tug one of the flowers free from the vine, then without climbing back down she put her lips to the narrow end of the orange blossom and blew.

BLAAATTTPH! HOOONK-APLTH!

"What are you . . ." I started to ask, but Lin shushed me and held a hand to her ear as she listened for something in the Microterium.

I listened, too, and soon a wonderful sound came to my ears.

HONK-HOOOOOOONK!

"Lin, you are a genius!" I said. I jumped up in the air and whooped real loud, calling back to Honk-Honk.

BLUURP-PAH! HOOOONK-A-SPLATCH! Lin blatted on her flower-trumpet again.

HONK-HOOOOOOONK! Honk-Honk honked back, sounding closer this time for sure.

"You are a horrible trumpet player, but—I said it before and I'll say it again. Lin, you are a GENIUS!"

Then, sloshing their way through the river were three very familiar Microsaur faces. Zip-Zap was leading the way, followed by Bruno, a lovable three-horned tiny-ceratops, and bringing up the rear was Honk-Honk, the hardest-working Microsaur in the whole Microterium.

Lin climbed down from the vine and stood right next to me. She wore the orange flower-trumpet like an overgrown party hat and smiled wide, knowing she was the smartest girl in the Microterium.

The Microsaurs sniffed at us, inspected the large egg, and stomped around in the mud to show us how happy they were to see us again.

"Hey, Honk-Honk, can we borrow your back?" Lin asked, and Honk-Honk honked. Lin looked at me with the silly flower hat on her head. "I think that means yes."

"For sure. And let me just say it again. Lin Song, you are a genius," I said.

"Took you long enough to figure it out, science-boy," Lin said as she tossed the flower to Bruno, who gobbled it up in one bite.

CHAPTER 8
SADDLE UP

Tying a gigantic oval egg to the back of a Microsaur isn't as easy as it sounds. We used all the yarn from the hammock to wrap it around the egg and Honk-Honk's belly. We had enough rope to make it all the way around six times, but on the seventh time around we came up a little short.

"Oh man, it's so close to wrapping around one more time," Lin said as she straddled the egg and tried to make the two loose ends meet. "Maybe we could weave some grass into a rope or something?"

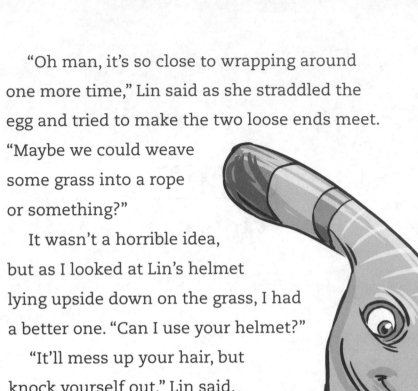

It wasn't a horrible idea, but as I looked at Lin's helmet lying upside down on the grass, I had a better one. "Can I use your helmet?"

"It'll mess up your hair, but knock yourself out," Lin said.

"It's not for me. It's for the egg," I said.

"Oh yeah. Good idea," Lin said as I tossed it up to her. By tying the ends of the yarn to the straps of her helmet, there was just enough room to complete the seventh loop of rope. "It worked!" Lin said.

"Is it stable?" I asked.

Lin was still next to the egg, and she rocked it back and forth. It didn't budge an inch, and Lin smiled down at me. "It's perfect. Well, almost perfect."

"Am I missing something? It looks good from down here," I said.

"You're not missing anything, but the egg is," Lin said. "Do you have a marker in your backpack?"

"Of course. I have a pack of four permanent markers in the side pocket. Why?" I asked.

"Toss one up for me, will ya? You'll see what's missing soon enough," Lin said. She snapped the cap off of the black marker, leaned over the egg while still sitting on top of it, and started drawing on the egg. She finished, then jumped down from Honk-Honk to inspect her masterpiece.

"Now it's perfect," Lin said with her hands on her hips and the marker tucked behind her ear. She had drawn a face on the egg, right under the helmet.

"Lin, I have to admit, that is much better," I
said. I pulled my backpack down tight over my
shoulders. "You ready to roll?"

"Yup. Race you to the Fruity Stars Lab?" she
asked as Zip-Zap, the fastest and wildest ride,
nudged her in the back. Zip-Zap loved taking
Lin for a ride almost as much as Lin loved
riding him.

"Do you remember how to get
there?" I asked Lin.

Lin jumped up on Zip-Zap's feathery back, then pointed in the totally wrong direction. "To the Fruity Stars Lab!" she said.

"Um. You should probably follow me or you'll end up in Maze Canyon," I said. I climbed up on Bruno's back. He was a much safer ride, and holding on to the crest of a triceratops almost felt like holding on to a steering wheel. I squeezed Bruno's ribs with my knees. "Let's go, Bruno. Up the hill, buddy!"

"I've always wanted to see Maze Canyon," Lin said, then she gave Zip-Zap a pat on his head, and they were off.

Honk-Honk followed us, but Zip-Zap and Lin took off in the opposite direction. I could hear her laughing as she bounced on the Microsaur's back, trying to get him to turn around and follow us to Professor Penrod's laboratory hideout, the Fruity Stars Lab.

"I guess you better call for them, Honk-Honk," I said.

Honk-Honk honked a long HOOOOOOOOONK, and before we got to the top of the hill, Lin

and Zip-Zap had not only caught up to us, they ran around us in circles, jumped off the trunks of trees, did flips over boulders, and splashed in mud puddles, and they were still faster than me and Bruno.

When we got to the top of a big hill, I looked down and saw the Fruity Stars Lab in the valley below us, but something wasn't quite right. Bruno was acting nervous, turning his wide, three-horned head to the left, then to the right. His usual happy wagging tail was curled up underneath him, and he kind of crouched down close to the ground. Something was bothering Honk-Honk, too, but I couldn't see anything.

I heard Lin and Zip-Zap running around, laughing and chirping with every bounce, then all of a sudden that stopped, too. All I could hear was the wind combing its way through the deep grass. Honk-Honk raised up on her back legs and sniffed the air. Then I heard a low, growling, clicking noise in the deep grass. Then another. AND ANOTHER.

I could feel Bruno's thick hide tremble underneath me. "It's okay, boy," I said in a soft voice, trying to calm the bulky Microsaur down, but it was no use.

I looked at Honk-Honk, and I could tell she was worried, too. Scared even. We were surrounded by growling and clicking, then Honk-Honk let out the loudest HOOOOOOOOOOOOOOOOOOONK I had ever heard.

It was just the boost Bruno needed. He bolted forward so fast that I nearly fell off. We ran right past Lin and Zip-Zap. "Come on! Get to the lab!" I shouted, and Lin yahooed cowgirl style as she gave Zip-Zap a tight squeeze with her legs. The four of us bolted toward the Fruity Stars Lab and ran inside. Lin and I jumped off our Microsaurs, then quickly knocked over the pencils holding up the entry flap.

There was barely enough room inside the lab for Lin and me, let alone two large, excited Microsaurs. I looked around and noticed that the place was a mess. There were strips of cardboard all around, and the walls were scratched and torn apart.

"The new pack beat us here, and they ripped the place to shreds," Lin said.

"We'll worry about that later. Where's Honk-Honk?" I asked, looking out a rough-edged hole ripped in the side of the Fruity Stars Lab.

"There she is," Lin said, stuffing her arm out of another hole and pointing up the hill.

Honk-Honk ran toward us, the egg bouncing on her back. A few of the ropes we'd tied on were dangling at her side, but even that didn't worry me as much as what I saw next.

The pack of tiny-raptors was chasing her down the hill. They had long, ostrich-like legs, thick black claws, and dark, speckled feathers.

Their wide eyes were separated by a big bony lump above their noses, and their mouths were filled with sharp, cardboard-shredding TEETH!

"RUN, HONK-HONK! RUN!" Lin shouted.

"We need to make room for her in here," I said, but it was no use. There wasn't enough room for a Shrink-A-Fied bag of jelly beans inside the lab with us, let alone a massive hadrosaur with an egg tied to her back.

But in the end, it didn't matter, because there was no stopping Honk-Honk. I was afraid she was going to run right into us, smashing down the Fruity Stars Lab in the process. Lin pulled her arm inside the box, and we both closed our eyes and hunkered down under a table made of dice, pushpins, and a big pink eraser. The ground beneath us shook like an earthquake, then as soon as it started, the shaking ended.

Honk-Honk had led the pack away, leaving us safely behind.

"That was pretty scary," I said after things had quieted down.

"Are you kidding? That was amazing. Did you see those little guys? They were ADORABLE! What were they, Danny?" she asked, but I was already on it.

"I'm not sure that word means what you think it means," I said as I jumped up and squeezed past Bruno. He grunted happily as he ate the pink corner off Professor Penrod's eraser table. I pulled down one of Professor Penrod's leather-bound notebooks from a bookshelf over his workbench. "Kittens are adorable, Lin," I said as I thumbed through the pages. "I know I've seen these in here before."

"What are you looking for?" Lin asked.

I found the right page, then turned and showed it to Lin. "This. And it isn't good news."

"Oh yeah. That's them all right. Toothy grin, long fingernails, fluffy little tails. See, they are adorable," Lin said.

"Well, these adorable little guys are oviraptors," I said.

"Ovi-what-ers?"

"Oviraptors. Egg thieves," I said. "And they are hungry."

"Oh, they are NOT stealing my blue-speckled egg!"

Lin said, then pushed Zip-Zap toward the door of the Fruity Stars Lab.

"I totally agree, but there are a lot of them. We're going to need a plan," I said.

Lin lifted the flap and let the sunshine in the lab with us. Bruno launched for the opening, nearly pushing her over on his way. "All right. Let's plan, but it better include teaching those oviraptors a lesson. Eating an extra-large, blue-speckled egg that never hurt anyone ever in its entire life is just rude."

I leaned against the workbench and scratched my chin as I thought real hard. I needed a plan, and I needed one fast. There were at least ten of the tiny-raptors, and they weren't going to be fooled by the tiny corn-dog trick again. And Lin was right. We needed to do more than just keep them away from the egg. We needed to train them to eat something else. This wasn't going to be the last egg in the Microterium. In fact, there was a good chance that somewhere tucked away in the swamp, or the desert canyons, or maybe even close to us in the deep weeds, there was a Microsaur sitting on her nest right now.

"Earth to Danny! We need to hurry or we won't find these guys," Lin said. She was sitting on Zip-Zap's back, doing everything she could to keep the jumpy Microsaur from bolting away.

I pulled out my smartphone and launched the SpyZoom app. I tapped on the GPS tracker button and a little red dot blinked on my screen. "Don't worry. We won't lose them. Honk-Honk is wearing a tracker," I said.

"Really?" Lin asked.

"Yeah. Remember? We stitched a Micro-GPS Beacon in your helmet. The very same helmet you tied to the egg," I said.

"Oh yeah. That little thing has come in handy more than once," Lin said.

Lin was right. The Micro-GPS Beacon had been super helpful in the Microterium. In fact, it's how we found the place when Twiggy, a tiny-dactyl who loved to collect shiny objects, stole it from the front of Lin's helmet before flying back to her nest. We used the tracking device on my phone to follow her to the Microterium, but after that adventure I decided to keep it out of sight so Twiggy wouldn't steal it again. Now it was hidden away, stuffed inside the liner of Lin's skateboarding helmet, which was currently getting a ride on Honk-Honk's back.

"So, what are we waiting for? Let's go get them!" Lin said.

"I have another idea. I'm not sure it will work, but if it does, we might be in for one exciting ride," I said.

"I'm in!" Lin said.

"Don't you want to hear my plan first?" I asked.

"Nope. As soon as you said 'exciting ride' I was ready to go," Lin said.

"All right. Step one, make me big again. Step two, I'll meet you, Zip-Zap, and Bruno at the bottom of the metal step," I said.

"Okay. You stand under the Grow-Hose, and I'll fire up the Expand-O-Matic," Lin said, and a rumbly feeling stirred around inside me, because I knew we were off on another amazing adventure.

CHAPTER 9
GEARING UP AND HEADING OUT

Shrinking 86.274 times your size in less than five seconds is incredible, but if you ask me, growing 86.274 times bigger is even better. The icy, glittery feeling is replaced with a warm, sparkly feeling that makes the back of my head itch for some reason. And instead of the snowflake feeling, you feel like you are a firework and someone just lit your fuse!

We'd used the Shrink-A-Fier and the Expand-O-Matic every day since we met Professor Penrod, but this time was different. This was the first time I'd grown while Lin stayed small.

Lin came running out of the Fruity Stars Lab, waving her arms and jumping up and down. She was saying something, but I couldn't quite hear what she said.

"What? I can't hear you!" I shouted.

Lin covered her ears and fell to her

bottom. I guess my voice was super loud to her now that I was big, which made sense when I stopped to think about it.

Lin stood and started acting out a scene, playing the world's smallest game of charades. She pointed to me and then to herself. She walked around, trying to act like she was huge, which was pretty funny being that she was smaller than a ladybug. Then she lowered her hand to the ground and made a "come here" motion. Then she made a walking motion with the fingers of her left hand, and used them to climb on her right hand, and I got it!

"Oh, you want a ride," I said, and she covered her ears again. "Oh, sorry," I whispered.

And it was a great idea. Why have Lin, Zip-Zap, and Bruno walk all the way to our meeting spot when I could just carry them? I bent down and placed my hand on the ground. Lin jumped on Zip-Zap's back and drove him onto my hand.

Bruno was busy tearing apart a red mushroom he'd found behind the Fruity Stars Lab. I very carefully lifted him up by his bony crest, then placed him in the palm of my hand.

Lin gave me the thumbs-up sign, and we were off. I held out my hand as I took three large steps, one over the hill next to the Fruity Stars Lab, one to cross the river and grassy plains, and the last one put me on the metal step in the old barn lab.

"How was that?" I whispered. But Lin was too busy laughing and cheering to reply. Her cheers sounded like the tiniest mouse in the world singing an opera.

I placed Lin and the Microsaurs in the grass below the step, then went on to phase two of my plan.

I rummaged around in Professor Penrod's barn lab until I found a bottle of rubber glue. I opened the lid and gave it a sniff. It looked and smelled all right, and I thought it would totally do the trick. Then I went on to phase three, which was by far the riskiest of the steps. And it came with a theory. I wasn't sure it would work, but my dad always says every good decision begins with a good theory. A question. An idea filled with wonder.

My wonder-filled idea was this: I knew that

standing below the Shrinker-Sprinkler for five seconds would shrink you, and anything you carried, exactly 86.274 times smaller than your original size. But what would happen if you held it under the Shrinker-Sprinkler for less than five seconds? I did some calculations in my notebook,

CPRs For 5 seconds = 86.274 x smaller

2X Too Big

CPRs For 2.5 seconds = 43.137 x smaller

PERFECT FIT!

then gathered up the upgrade parts from *The Bolt*, which were still scattered on the floor next to the package that once held an egg and a pack of egg stealers. If my math was right, I needed to shrink the parts 43.137 times smaller, which should take exactly 2.5 seconds.

Lucky for me, I had already studied the plans for Professor Penrod's Shrink-A-Fier and I knew exactly what to do. I just needed to adjust the timer and give it a try. I placed the car parts and the bottle of rubber glue on the metal step, adjusted the timer, then jumped on the step to trigger the Shrink-A-Fier. Just before the glittery CRPs fell on me, I jumped off the metal step and watched as the glue and RC car upgrades shrank exactly 43.137 times their original size.

"Perfect!" I shouted. There's almost nothing I love as much as having a theory work the first time. I carefully lowered the preshrunk parts and the glue on the grass next to Lin, Zip-Zap, and

Bruno, then I put the timer back to five seconds and shrank myself for the second time that day.

By the time I climbed down from the metal step, I could see that Lin was way ahead of me. She was using the glue to stick the Sonic-Earth Shaker part to Bruno's rump.

I ran to join them. "So, do you think it will work?"

"For sure." The bottle of glue was almost as big as Lin, and she had a big boogery lump of rubber muck stuck in her hair. "And you were right. This is going to be a heck of a fun ride. We're totally going to teach those oviraptors a lesson they won't soon forget. But there's a problem, Danny. A big one," she said.

"What's that?" I asked.

"I'm going to need these upgrades to teach someone else a lesson in less than three hours. Remember? Icky Vicky goes down at four forty-five," she said.

"Don't worry. We're just testing these out for now. We'll have plenty of time to attach them back onto *The Bolt* before the race," I said.

"We better, or I'm in big trouble," Lin said.

I lifted up the Goo-Cannon to test its weight. It was heavy, but I thought I could carry it while riding Bruno. Lin dunked the back end of the Grappling-Grabber in the glue, then stuck it to her shirt. She plucked a few pieces of grass and started weaving a belt. Before I was able to convince Zip-Zap that gluing a Slap-Clapper to his back was a good idea, Lin had tied her new grass belt around the Grappling-Grabber and her waist and pulled it tight.

"Hey, Danny. I bet we look totally cool right now," Lin said.

"Heck, yes, we do. Wait. I have one last idea before we go," I said. I set a timer on my phone, then wedged it in a flower as tall as my dad. "Quick. Come over here and say cheese!"

We looked ready for battle, which was good because there was no telling how hungry the oviraptors would be by the time we found them.

"Let's go rescue that egg!" I said. With the Goo-Cannon in my arms, I ran and jumped on Bruno's back, stuffing myself between his crest and the Sonic-Earth Shaker glued to his butt.

Lin whooped, then hurdled onto Zip-Zap and headed straight for the Fruity Stars Lab.

"Boy, Bruno. That girl could get lost in a one-room house," I said, and I can't say for sure, but I swear my three-horned friend laughed at my joke.

CHAPTER 10
TRACKING DOWN TROUBLE

By the time Lin discovered she was going in the wrong direction, Bruno and I had made our way through the grass fields that stretched out below the big metal step. She caught up to us as we arrived at a boggy swamp. Bruno seemed right at home in the gooey mud and black water, but Zip-Zap did not enjoy it at all.

Eventually the ground dried up and we made our way to a thick, overgrown jungle full of mushrooms the size of trees, and moss so thick and green it looked like frosting.

"We're catching up to them," I said as I checked my GPS tracker. "We'll be in Maze Canyon as soon as we get out of this mushroom forest. We should meet up with Honk-Honk and the oviraptors there."

"And the egg," Lin said.

"Right. And the egg," I said.

"Then let's hurry!" Lin said. She cheered on Zip-Zap, and her springy Microsaur spurted forward, jumped on the soft top of a smaller mushroom, then trampolined high into the air.

Bruno trampled on, smooshing moss between his big, wide toes. Before long the soft green earth turned to sand the color of a sunset. Bright orangish-red rocks stood up on the landscape, and cactus plants dotted the area like nature's pincushions.

The sand in front of us was covered in footprints. One set of large Honk-Honk prints, followed by a pack of three-toed tiny-raptor prints. I couldn't see Lin, but I could see Zip-Zap's large prints in the sand as well.

I pulled up the GPS to take another look, but I didn't need it because Honk-Honk HOOOONKED ahead in the red rock canyons and I knew exactly where to go.

"DANNY! I found them!" Lin yelled, her voice echoing on the large rock walls, and I nudged Bruno to run as fast as he could.

We entered Maze Canyon, and the tall rock walls seemed to reach up and touch the sky. The canyon twisted and turned, making it impossible to see what was around the next corner. It was easy to tell why Professor Penrod had given it the name Maze Canyon. If it weren't for the footprints in the sandy floor, it would be easy to get lost.

"Come on, Bruno, old boy. Let's catch up," I said. Bruno was panting pretty hard and I could tell he was ready for a rest, but I knew it would take more than a little run through the Microterium to wear out this tiny-ceratops.

We squeezed through a narrow spot where the canyon walls rubbed Bruno's wide crest on both sides, then the canyon opened up to an area so big you could easily hold a soccer tournament in the flat, sandy space. But there were no soccer games that day, only Honk-Honk being chased by a pack of tiny-raptors, who were being chased by Lin and Zip-Zap.

"Get as close as you can," I shouted to Lin as I grabbed my smartphone and launched the SpyZoom app. It was hard to see the screen as I bounced along on Bruno's back. I scrolled through the test upgrades menu and found the controls for the Slap-Clapper.

"Sic 'em, Zip-Zap!" Lin yelled. Zip-Zap lowered his head, pointed his beak toward the raptor pack, and let out a loud CAAAAW!

Zip-Zap stretched out his neck, then took a big bite, chomping his jaws down on a mouthful of oviraptor tail feathers. He whipped the little guy right out of the running, flinging it out into the sandy desert, where it flopped head over claws until it rolled to a stop.

It was so much fun to watch Zip-Zap make his way up into the pack that I almost forgot to do my job. When Zip-Zap caught up to the middle of the pack, I tapped the button to extend the Slap-Clapper hands. Mechanical arms

reached out on either side of Zip-Zap, but the big birdlike Microsaur didn't slow down one bit.

"Fire, Danny! FIRE!" Lin shouted, giddy with excitement.

I launched the right hand first, and it swung down low and slapped an oviraptor right out of the pack. It rolled into a cactus patch, then jumped straight up into the air, its rear end full

of spiky cactus needles. Then I unloaded the left hand. It swooped down in front of Zip-Zap, plowing two of the hungry critters right over, where they toppled and rolled before they came up spitting mouthfuls of sand. The pack of ten oviraptors was down to six.

"Direct hit!" Lin shouted. She waved her arms up and down, and Zip-Zap copied her and the two took flight for a few seconds. Watching Lin ride Zip-Zap was like watching two really good dancers glide across the dance floor. Lin held on to Zip-Zap, no problem, but the Slap-Clapper had had enough. The glue just wasn't strong enough, and it slipped from his back, where it fell, half buried in the sand.

"Danny!" Lin shouted. "We're going to need that!"

"It's okay. We still have plenty of upgrades!" I shouted back.

Bruno and I were falling behind, his tree-trunk-shaped legs unable to keep up with the other Microsaurs. Then I saw a shortcut that had excellent goo potential written all over it. The wide canyon we were running in was narrowing to a dead end. Two large rocks shaped like overgrown marshmallows were soon going to force the herd of running Microsaurs to take a sharp turn. I cranked Bruno to the left, knowing that if we hurried we could cut them off and maybe stop a few more of the tiny-raptors.

There was only one thing in our way: a wall of prickly cacti. Bruno wasn't the fastest runner in the Microterium, but he sure was good at smashing things. I wasn't too excited about riding a Microsaur through a cactus field, but

I knew the prickly plants wouldn't slow Bruno down.

He lowered his head, and I ducked behind his hard crest just in time. Bruno trampled through the cacti, sending cactus parts flying everywhere and not getting one scratch on him. Or on me!

The plan worked great, and I slid from Bruno's back and came to a stop at the edge of a small ravine in the canyon floor. Sure enough, just as I had thought, Honk-Honk rounded the corner around the two marshmallow-shaped rocks and sprinted down the little slot canyon. Six snappy Microsaurs chased after her, yanking at the hammock ropes that held the egg in place.

Lin was catching up to Honk-Honk, passing the Microsaurs one by one. She was in the middle of the pack when I yelled for her to "DUCK!"

Lin obeyed just as I tapped a button to launch a stream of black, sludgy goo out of the

Goo-Cannon. It squirted over her head and splattered all over the four slowest oviraptors. The tiny-raptors were covered in gooey gunk, and soon they were so glopped down that they stopped and started immediately trying to clean one another off.

"Bull's-eye!" I shouted. "Come on, Bruno! We've got this now!"

I had used every ounce of the goo, so I dropped the Goo-Cannon in the sand. I made a mental note to come back and get it later. Bruno ran

to me and I jumped on without him needing to slow down.

Lin and I caught up to Honk-Honk in a winding canyon, but the last two oviraptors got lost in the twisting canyon and fell behind. We yelled at Honk-Honk to stop, but

she kept on running, until the worst possible thing happened. We found a dead end.

Honk-Honk stopped, sucking in big, deep puffs of air. The hammock that was holding the

egg on her back was a total mess. Long strands of yellow rope dangled all around, and it seemed like the only thing holding it on was the yarn Lin had tied to her helmet.

Sitting on Bruno's back, I listened carefully for signs of the oviraptors, but aside from a lot of heavy breathing, the canyon was silent.

"Do you think they gave up?" Lin asked.

"I doubt it. I don't think they are the giving-up type," I said.

Something growled and I looked at Lin with my eyes wide.

"Don't worry. It was my stomach. I'm starving," she said, but that wasn't all it was. I heard the growl again, followed by the clicking sound that was really starting to get on my nerves.

CHAPTER 11
CORNERED

Two very unhappy, snarling tiny-raptors crept around the canyon bend. Their heads were held low, and their arms were stretched out. I recognized the leader of the pack, the biggest oviraptor, with its wide crest and blue tongue. They stepped out into the sun and stared at us. Then things went from bad to mega-bad.

"Uh-oh, Danny. We're outnumbered," Lin said as four oviraptors covered in black goo joined the pack.

Honk-Honk started to fidget, rubbing her back against the rock cliff wall. The ropes that held the egg in place were about to come loose. "It's all right, Honk-Honk. Everything is going to be fine," I said, although I didn't believe it myself. I knew we were trapped.

A raptor with a rear end filled with cactus needles squawked as it ran around the corner, followed by two others who had met the Slap-Clapper just minutes ago, and they did NOT look pleased.

"We have to do something, Danny!" Lin shouted. She held her skateboard in front of her like a shield.

I was getting worried, too, but we only had two upgrades left. "I have an idea, but . . ." I said.

"But what? Are you worried about the race?

I'd rather have that egg safe than have enough upgrades to beat Vicky. Use it, Danny. Teach these guys a lesson," Lin said.

The Sonic-Earth Shaker was still glued to Bruno, and I tossed Lin my phone. The last of the tiny-raptor pack snuck around the corner. Its tail

feathers were missing and it stared at Zip-Zap, looking ready for revenge.

"When I say fire, hit the button labeled S-ES, then cover your ears," I said.

There was a large pile of rocks stacked on top of the cliff edge between us and the oviraptors. I wasn't sure the sound waves from the Sonic-Earth Shaker would be enough to bust them free, but I knew it was our only chance. I turned Bruno around, aiming his rump and the Sonic-Earth Shaker at the base of the rocks, and yelled.

"FIRE!"

Lin hit the button and the upgrade BOOOOOMED, sending out a pulse of sound so strong it knocked me back ten feet. Bruno didn't budge as sand blew through the air, creating a curtain of dry, reddish-brown dust between us and the tiny-raptors. For a moment I couldn't hear anything except my heartbeat. Then I heard Lin, Zip-Zap, Bruno, and Honk-Honk celebrating.

I stood and shook my head, sand pouring down from my hair. I saw why they were cheering. The Sonic-Earth Shaker worked perfectly! Not only had it brought down the stack of rocks, but it had blasted a hole in the canyon wall so big it would be easy for us to escape. The dead end was dead no more, and there was a pile of rubble between us and the oviraptors that would keep them away for good. We were finally safe.

"Did you see that? What a great shot, Bruno!" Lin said. She ran over and gave Bruno a kiss right on the nose, and he grinned. My ears were ringing and I was as hungry as a pack of oviraptors. I looked at Honk-Honk. She looked happy as she rested in the deep, warm sand. I was ready to sit and have some lunch and enjoy our victory, but something was missing.

"Where's the egg?" I asked.

"It's right . . . uh-oh." Lin pointed at

Honk-Honk. Lin's helmet was lying upside down in the sand next to Honk-Honk, but the egg was no longer on her back. "It was there a second ago."

I turned around and saw the egg, balanced dangerously over a dark black hole in the ground. Right away I knew it was the entrance to an underground cave.

"There it is." I dropped the Sonic-Earth Shaker in the sand and started walking toward the egg. Lin joined me, and the egg started to teeter. "STOP!" I hissed.

Lin stopped mid-step, balancing on one foot like a tiptoeing flamingo. "Why are we stopping?" she whispered.

"Because the egg is going to fall into that cave if we take another step. It's only barely balanced on the edge, and I'm afraid if we take one more step it will roll in," I said quietly.

"Should I use the Grappling-Grabber?" Lin asked. It was still glue-tied to her back.

I thought about it, but before I could decide, Bruno made my mind up for me. He sneezed, blowing a slobbery dust storm in the air that knocked the egg right down the hole.

"No!!!" Lin yelled. She threw me my smartphone, dropped her skateboard, and dove into the hole. After tucking my phone safely away, I quickly yanked two flashlights from my backpack. I had a feeling we were going to need them, and I wasn't giving up. We'd gone too far to lose the egg now.

CHAPTER 12

BENEATH THE MICROTERIUM

I wasn't the jumping-into-a-dark-hole type, so I poked my head into the mouth of the cave. I could hear rushing water below. I shined the flashlight down into the hole. Icicle-shaped stalactites and stalagmites were all around, growing drop by drop as the rich minerals of the Microterium leaked through the earth's floor. An

old, rusty steam pipe stretched through the cave ceiling, and a river of dark water gurgled and flowed downstream. But I couldn't see Lin or the egg. Then I heard her voice coming up from the hole in the ground.

"Danny-ny-ny?" Lin's voice echoed in the dark of the cave. "Help meee-mee-me!"

"Where are you-oo-oo?" I echoed back.

"I'm in the river-iver-iver!" she shouted from deep inside the cave. "Just jump in. The water is warm!"

The beam from my flashlight carved into the black and saw my soggy best friend holding on to a yellow strand of yarn tied around a great big egg.

"I'm coming-ing-ing!" I shouted. I rolled up my sleeves, held both flashlights tight in my hands, then jumped into the dark hole, hoping that I'd land in the slow-moving water.

The water was warm as I splashed around in the dark. Holding one flashlight over my head and one in my mouth, I found Lin. I swam to Lin, grabbed on to the yellow yarn, then passed her a waterproof flashlight. She put it in her mouth and said, "Hanks." We held on tight to the yarn as we floated downstream. Time crept by, but I had no way of knowing how long it had been. It's easy to lose track of time when you're coasting down an underground river. Eventually my feet bumped against the sandy river bottom.

I held on to the egg with one hand and took my flashlight in the other so I could talk. "It's getting shallower," I said to Lin.

"Aii hush hiii aaa, uh-uh ooo," Lin said back,

which I totally understood. She had just hit the bottom, too.

The narrow beam from my flashlight shined to the right and I saw a little sandy riverbank in the cave. I motioned to Lin, and in a few big, soggy steps, we were dragging the massive egg to a dry, if still pitch-black, beach.

We both fell on our backs, exhausted.

Lin spit out her flashlight and sighed.

I knew exactly how she felt. I was finished running for the day, hungry, soaked, and ready for a nap.

"Hey, Danny," Lin said in the dark.

"Yeah?"

"Is there any chance your backpack is waterproof?" she asked.

"Of course. There's important stuff in there," I said.

"Important stuff like half-frozen pizza and corn dogs?" she said.

"At this very moment I can't think of anything more important," I said. Then we both started laughing in the warm, dark cave.

CHAPTER 13
WHAT'S FOR LUNCH?

I burrowed to the bottom of my backpack, then handed the pizza and corn dogs to Lin. Everything inside the pack, including my smartphone, was nice and dry. It was dark inside the cave, but with my four flashlights buried in the sand, pointing up to the ceiling, and my phone screen glowing it wasn't too bad.

Lin draped the last slices of pizza and two corn dogs on the top of the steam pipe, and before long the whole cave smelled delicious.

"I'm going to save this last corn dog for later. Who knows how long we'll be in here?" Lin said.

She handed me the corn dog and I stuffed it back in my pack.

"Good idea," I said as I tried to find out on my phone where we were.

"So, exactly how lost are we, Mr. Maps?" Lin asked as she slumped down next to me on the sandy floor of the cave.

"Oh boy. I'm really not sure. I'd say we're somewhere between kind of lost and totally, buried-under-a-secret-lab-while-Shrink-A-Fied-to-the-size-of-ants lost," I said.

"Oh boy is right," Lin said. "At least we aren't being chased by oviraptors anymore. There is that."

"Yup. There is that."

"So . . . what do we do now?" Lin asked.

"We eat some lunch, because we need food to make our brains work. Then we make a plan and get out of this cave," I said.

"Sounds good. But I know what we can do while we wait. We can sit on the egg," Lin said.

"I'm too tired to sit on an egg," I said.

Lin stood up, then held out a hand to help me up, too. "Come on. We can just hug it, then. I think it needs us," she said. I gave her my hand and she pulled me up.

Lin hugged one side of the beat-up egg, and I leaned against the other. I put my cheek right up next to the shell. The water of the cave had warmed it up, and it felt nice against my face. We were only standing there for a few seconds when something inside moved.

"Did you feel that?" Lin asked. I could hear the happiness in her voice.

"I sure did. I think something's happening," I said, then a crack zigzagged down the middle of the egg and a little claw reached out and wiggled in the air.

"I think it's happening NOW! I'm going to be a mom!" Lin shouted. "Come on out, little guy. You're going to love it here in the Microterium."

The big egg cracked loudly, and Lin and I took a step back. A big chunk of shell fell to the ground, revealing a scaly body that twitched and squirmed.

Another crack, and a nose poked out.

"Holy micro-zoli! Are you seeing this?" I asked.

Another piece of shell fell away and a tail slipped from the egg and wagged slowly back and forth.

"This . . . is the greatest thing . . . I've seen in my entire life," Lin whispered.

"Yeah," I whispered back. "Same here."

The nose jabbed out through the shell a bit more, revealing an eye that blinked at us in the dark cave. It was hard to tell exactly what it was inside the egg, but I started to get a little jumbly feeling in my stomach. My insides were a mixture of nervous and a little bit scared, because I had an idea of what we were going to meet.

Then something really strange happened. Another claw stabbed through the egg toward the bottom. It tore a little hole in the shell, then another nose and two tiny nostrils shoved out and sniffed around.

"What is that?" Lin asked. "A two-headed Microsaur?"

Then, with a flick of two strong, leathery tails, and a kick of four powerful back legs, the rest of the eggshell fell away.

"TWINS!" Lin and I shouted at the same time.

The baby Microsaurs rolled around on the floor of the cave, crushing what was left of the eggshell beneath them. Then one of them tried to stand on its wobbly little legs. It bobbled around for a bit, then stood all by itself, using its

long tail for balance. It hobbled over to its twin
and nuzzled it with a wide nose, helping its egg-
mate stand for the first time.

"They are so magically, wonderfully, perfectly,
amazingly CUTE!" Lin said. "I can't help it.
I'm going to hug one." She bounced right up
to one of the twins and gave it a great big hug.

The new hatchling leaned its head against Lin's shoulder and cooed as it tried to hug her back with its tiny little arms.

"What are they, Danny? They don't look like oviraptors," she said.

"That's because they are not. They have huge feet. Powerful tails. Tiny eyes on big, squarish heads. And their arms are so little. Whoa! I mean. WOW! Lin, do you know what these are?" I asked.

The Microsaur was rubbing its big head up

against Lin's chin and making a deep, rumbly, purring noise in its tiny chest. Lin started laughing. The baby Microsaur nudged her and she fell over in the sand. "Whatever they are, they are strong."

"That's because these are the kings of the Microsaur kingdom. These are twin Tyrannosaurus rexes," I said as the other Microsaur approached me. It seemed to grin at me, and I reached out and scratched its nose. It closed its eyes and purred.

"You mean, *Microsaurus* rexes, Danny. They are still Microsaurs, remember?" Lin said.

The Microsaurus rex was only a tiny bit shorter than me, and it was less than a minute old. It tilted its head and looked at me through shiny yellow-and-black eyes. It opened its mouth and showed me a smile filled with bright white teeth. Then it let out the tiniest squeak ever. I giggled a little, and something about that noise made the tiny-saurus rex jump into action. It pushed me over and started licking my face.

I couldn't help it. I burst out laughing, because its rough tongue really tickled. Who knew a face could be ticklish?

"It likes me!" I said.

"No, Danny. It LOVES you!" Lin said.

Lin was standing again, and she used both of her hands to push up the corners of her Micro-rex's mouth into a big smile. This made her laugh so hard I thought she was going to pass out. "They are so much fun, Danny! Don't you just adore them with all your heart?" she said.

"I do," I said, "but this little guy needs a breath mint."

"They need something. I bet they are starving. What do baby Microsaurs eat? Microsaur milk?" Lin asked.

I wiggled away from my newborn lick-a-saurus and stood up. I scratched it under the chin, and it closed its eyes and purred again.

"No. I mean, I'm sure they would drink milk, but I'm guessing they'd eat just about anything really. Only mammals drink milk as newborns. Reptiles and birds, and Microsaurs for that matter, eat pretty much what their parents eat," I said.

"Oh yeah. That's right. I saw this one show where the momma bird chewed up some worms, then barfed them into the baby bird's mouth," Lin said. "We need to find some worms."

"Are you going to chew them up first?" I asked. Lin grabbed a flashlight and started shining it around the cave.

"There's got to be some worms in this cave. Help me look, Danny," Lin said.

"But you didn't answer me. Are you going to pre-chew a worm for your tiny-saurus rex?" I asked.

"Wait. Did you say MY tiny-saurus rex? Do you mean I get to keep it?" she asked. "Because if that's the case, I'll chew and barf up anything in the world if I get to keep it."

I laughed as I helped Lin search for worms for the baby Microsaurs. "That's so gross," I said. "But I totally believe you'd do it."

"Oh, I would. A mother's got to do what a mother's got to do," Lin said.

While we searched for worms or something else to feed the baby Microsaurs, the two curious rexes took matters into their own hands. Well, into their mouths, that is.

Lin swung her flashlight over to the steam pipe that was warming up our pizza and corn dogs. "Hey, look at that. Mine already found something to eat and I didn't even have to chew it up first," she said. And sure enough, Lin's tiny-saurus rex was snarfing down one of the two corn dogs.

Lin ran over to her Micro-rex and patted it on the head. "Wasn't that a tasty treat, Cornelia?" she said.

"Cornelia?" I asked. Lin tossed me the second corn dog so I could feed my tiny-saurus rex.

"Yeah. You are what you eat. But I couldn't call her corn dog. So . . . Cornelia," Lin said, which sounded perfectly logical to me.

"Well, I guess I'll call mine Cornhowser, then. Here's one for you, boy," I said as I offered the half-warm corn dog to my new friend.

The tiny-saurus rex sniffed the corn dog, then wrinkled his nose and stuck out his tongue.

"What?" Lin said. "Have you ever met a T. rex that doesn't like corn dogs?"

"Ummm, just one, I guess," I said.

I took a bite of the corn dog to show him that it was safe. "Yummm. So good. You should try this, Cornhowser. It's delicious. Could use a squirt of mustard, but it's still really good."

The Microsaur turned up his nose and looked at me as if I was trying to feed him rotten socks for lunch. "Here, you can give this one to

Cornelia. I guess this guy isn't hungry." I tossed the corn dog toward Lin, and Cornelia jumped up and caught it in the air, swallowing it whole, stick and all.

"Whoa! Did you see that?" Lin asked. "Who's

a good girl?" Lin scratched Cornelia's belly and the baby Microsaur smiled, then burped a gassy cloud of corn-dog air, which made Lin laugh.

Lin and Cornelia rolled and played in the sand as I watched the other twin sniff the air. He was searching around for something else to eat, and I certainly hoped that he wasn't searching for a science-loving boy to munch for lunch.

He rolled over a rock and sniffed at whatever was hiding beneath it, not finding anything worth a lick. Then he sniffed at my backpack, nearly shoving me over with his strong, square nose.

"There's nothing in there worth eating, buddy," I said. "I mean, there's one last corn dog, but we both know those aren't your thing."

Then he raised up high on his powerful back legs and got a big, deep sniff of something great, and I knew exactly what he wanted. Only the greatest food ever invented: a perfect triangle of bready goodness, covered with sauce, cheese, and pepperoni.

The Microsaurus rex followed his nose to the back of the steam pipe, where he gobbled up the two pieces of pizza in two big bites.

"Pizza!" I said, and Lin looked up at me.

"What did you say?" she asked.

"Pizza. His name is Pizza," I said.

The pizza-loving Microsaur jumped up and down, wagged his tail, and rubbed his tummy with his tiny

arms, and I knew right away that I had found the perfect name for my new friend.

Then before I even had a chance to worry about what Lin and I were going to eat for lunch, something above our heads started scratching. Dust fell from the ceiling of the cave and Pizza and Cornelia ran to hide behind us, scared of the strange noise.

"What is that?" Lin asked.

A little piece of the cave dropped down and thumped me on the shoulder and, without saying a word, Lin and I took a few steps back.

The scratching stopped for a minute, and we heard something that we did NOT want to hear. A low growling sound, followed by a clicking noise of a pack of very stubborn, very hungry tiny-raptors.

CHAPTER 14
A BIT OF LUCK

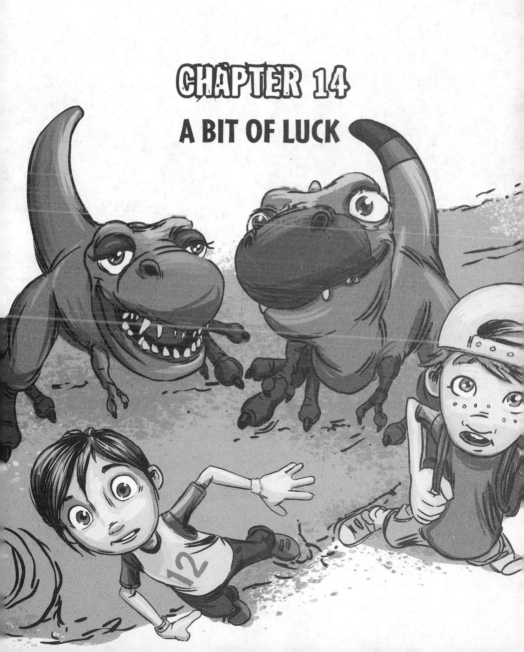

The first oviraptor to poke its head through the hole in the cave ceiling stuck its big, blue tongue out at us and licked the dirt off its snout. It looked around in the dark cave, and when it saw Lin and me holding our flashlights, it growled and clicked, and the rest of the pack clicked after him, their voices rattling in the ceiling, sending a shiver through my whole body.

"We need a plan, Danny," Lin said. "The best plan ever, or we are in real trouble."

"I'm thinking. But it's hard to think of something great when Mr. Blue Tongue is staring at you like you are a walking hamburger," I said.

Mr. Blue Tongue pulled his head back up into the ceiling, then started stomping in the hole that he and his pack were digging. At first they were all stomping at different times, and it didn't seem like they would ever get through the earth, but after a few scattered hops they all got on the same rhythm.

Thump! BUMP! BOOOM!

"I don't care for this one bit!" I said, and Pizza whined at my back.

"Maybe we should jump back in the river," Lin said as Cornelia cleared her throat and bared her teeth at the oviraptors' noise.

Thump! BUMP! BOOOOOOOM!

Then all at once an avalanche of rock, dirt, and tiny-raptors crashed down from above. Dust filled the air as a hole big enough to drive a car through opened above us. Sunshine stabbed in the hole, and I blinked and rubbed my eyes as I waited for them to adjust to the light.

When I could finally see again, I kind of wished that I couldn't. Because all I could see was hungry-looking oviraptors, all around us.

I was about to step forward and yell at them to move back, hoping that they would obey, but Pizza pushed in front of me. He growled and showed the oviraptors his shiny teeth. I looked over at Lin and saw that she was being protected by Cornelia, too. Even though the Microsaurus rexes were newborns they were coming to our rescue, snarling and growling and ready for a fight!

I looked up through the hole in the roof of the cave, and I saw something glorious. A brightly colored Fruity Stars cereal box.

"How about that plan, Danny?" Lin said.

"Sometimes all the planning in the world doesn't make up for a little bit of luck," I said to Lin. I pointed up at the Fruity Stars Lab. "You ready to use that Grappling-Grabber you've been lugging around?" I asked.

"SWEET! YES!" Lin said. She wrapped her arms around Cornelia, and I quickly launched the SpyZoom app on my phone. I swiped through the buttons until I found the Grappling-Grabber controls, then I called Pizza to my side.

Lin and I each locked an arm together and held on to our Microsaurs with the other. The pack of tiny-raptors was closing in tight. Mr. Blue Tongue chomped at the air like he was chewing an invisible steak, and I was ready to get out of there!

"Hold on tight!" I said. I pressed down on the Grappling-Grabber button, and the device glue-tied to Lin's back fired straight up into the back of the Fruity Stars Lab. Then I raised the retract lever on my phone all the way to full speed, and Lin, Cornelia, Pizza, and I were yanked out of the cave in a flash!

We tumbled to the soft, grass-covered ground, and the sunlight on my face never felt so good. But we didn't have time to sit and enjoy things, because we both knew that the oviraptors would be coming out of the cave any second.

"Quick. Get Pizza and Cornelia to the penny platform," I said, and Lin totally understood.

"We're taking them with us," she said as she started pushing the baby Microsaurs toward the side of the nearly destroyed Fruity Stars Lab.

"I'm not leaving them here until we figure out how to satisfy those oviraptors," I said as I ran inside the lab.

Professor Penrod had discovered that the copper pennies were the perfect conductor for his CEPs, Carbonic Expansion Particles. So, while the cold aluminum of the metal step was part of the Shrink-A-Fying process, the sun-warmed copper penny was the key to expanding back to normal size.

I cranked a few levers, twisted a few knobs, and sparked a flame beneath the soda can that Professor Penrod used to hold his CEP mixture. It didn't take long for the CEPs to start boiling up into the twisting tubes of the Expand-O-Matic, and I knew I had just enough time to run outside the lab and jump on the penny with Lin and the twins.

The showerhead above Lin dripped an orangish-golden drop and I lunged for the penny platform just as the Expand-O-Matic coughed out a puff of fine mist. Toasty-warm, golden particles danced all around us, glittering in the sunshine and sparkling against our skin.

I looked down to watch the ground shrink beneath me as Lin and I returned to our normal size. But Pizza and Cornelia almost disappeared as they stayed tiny, looking lost and afraid on the penny platform.

"Where's Cornelia?" asked Lin.

I picked up the penny, balancing the twins carefully on its shiny copper face. "They are right here. Perfectly safe and fine," I said. "Hold out your hand."

Lin did, and I tipped the coin and Cornelia slid into the palm of her hand. I placed Pizza in my hand before returning the penny to the Microterium.

"Oh my gosh, she's soooooo tiny!" Lin said. "Why didn't she grow?"

"She didn't need to. They are already regular-sized," I said. "The Expand-O-Matic doesn't make you bigger. It brings you back. This is as big as a Microsaur can get."

"Oh yeah," Lin said. "Which is fine with me, little cutie." Lin used the very tip of her finger to scratch under Cornelia's chin. I heard the tiniest squeak from my palm, and I smiled down at the micro-sized Pizza. He curled up in a ball and fell asleep. He'd had a long day, too.

"Are you ready to get out of here?" I asked.

"Almost. But I need that last corn dog in your backpack first," Lin said.

"Oh man. It's in pretty bad shape. Let's go get some fresh ones at my house," I explained.

"It's not for me," Lin said. She curled her hand around Cornelia, then unzipped my pack and pulled out the most smooshed, dirty, beat-up, sad-looking corn dog on the planet. "This looks perfect."

Lin leaned down and stuck the corn dog in the hole that led to the dark cave below the Fruity Stars Lab. She tilted her head and looked off into nothing as she held the corn-dog stick. "Almost ready," she said. "Just one more second."

One second turned into three, then five, then ten. She lifted the corn dog out of the hole and smiled big and wide as she inspected it. A pack of tiny-raptors clung to the bottom of the smashed-up corn dog.

"I'll be right back," Lin said. She took a few big, careful steps, carrying the corn dog and the hungry pack of tiny-raptors to the very back of the Microterium. I watched as she carefully placed the corn dog, which was about a hundred times bigger than the tiny-raptors, in the shade of a little bonsai tree, then stood and nodded down at what she had done.

"That ought to satisfy them for a while," she said.

"For sure," I said. I heard a little HOOONK-HOOOOOONK rising up from below and looked down at my feet. I looked over at Lin, who was carefully making her way back to me.

"Hey. Honk-Honk, Bruno, and Zip-Zap are back," I said. "Everything is back to normal."

Lin joined me and we looked down at our tiny friends and the completely destroyed empty box of cereal. "Well, not everything is back to normal. The Fruity Stars Lab has seen better days."

"Well, I guess we could try to fix it up. I think there's some supplies in the . . ." I was going to suggest a plan for rebuilding the Fruity Stars Lab when Lin shouted me right out of my train of thought.

"IT'S FOUR THIRTY-SIX! I bet Icky Vicky is blow-drying her hair right now! She'll be ready to race in no time!"

"Well then, what are we waiting for?" I said. "We've got work to do!"

CHAPTER 15
BACK TO THE TRACK

When you're so small you can use a pencil eraser as a beanbag chair, it takes a long time to travel through the lush landscape of the Microterium. The place is massive and filled with everything from live rivers and swamps to bone-dry canyons. The more Lin and I explored the place, the more amazed I was at how much time it must have taken Professor Penrod to build it.

But when you are regular-sized, it seems pretty small. I mean, I could run from one end of the old secret, hideaway barn to the other in a few seconds. It's the fastest way to travel, but it was almost impossible to do without crushing the carefully crafted landscape, not to mention the Microsaurs that lived there. There was only one place you could easily walk in the Microterium when you were regular-sized: the three stepping-stones Professor Penrod had placed between the Expand-O-Matic and the metal platform below the Shrink-A-Fier.

On our way back to the metal step, Lin reached down and picked up the world's smallest skateboard. It was right where she had left it earlier, between the Shrink-A-Fier and the first rock stepping-stone.

I wanted to quickly gather up the upgrade

parts we'd scattered throughout the Microterium as we dealt with the tiny-raptors, but we had to find a place for the twins first. I found a small glass jar and carefully placed Pizza inside it.

"Here. Hold this while I try to pick up the upgrades," I said as I passed the jar of Pizza to Lin. She added Cornelia in with her brother and the two tiny-saurus rexes snuggled up tight.

Standing on the wooden floor, careful not to press against the metal step and trigger the Shrink-A-Fier, I leaned out over the swamp and tried to reach The Bolt's upgrades that we'd left behind in the desert canyon.

"I can't reach," I said.

"Here, let me try," Lin said. She stood on the very edge of the barn-lab floor. "Grab my hand and lower me down."

Lin and I made a human chain as I lowered her down over the swamp. It only added a few inches, but she was able to grab the Slap-Clapper

and the Goo-Cannon. I pulled her back up to the step and she handed me the half-shrunk upgrades.

"Sorry, Danny. That's all I could reach," Lin said as I stared at the parts in my hand.

I checked my watch. The race was going to start in less than seven minutes. I tucked the tiny parts in my pocket, gave Lin a smile, and

shrugged. "Well, I guess we'll have to beat
Vicky the old-fashioned way. With good driving,"
I said.

"And the Hammer of Doom. Don't forget that,"
Lin said.

I looked back into Professor Penrod's secret
barn-lab, and there on the floor was the
destroyed package, *The Bolt*, and the Hammer of
Doom. The upgrade was in pretty bad shape, but
I thought I could turn it into something useful in
the next thirty seconds if I hurried.

"Okay. Here's the plan," I told Lin. "You make
someplace more permanent and cozy for Pizza
and Cornelia, and I'll turn that RC car into a
champion."

"Deal!" Lin said.

I shucked off my backpack, then fell to my
knees and started working on *The Bolt*. All of the
upgrades except for the Hammer of Doom were
still microsized, so my choices were limited. I

had really wanted to tweak the settings on the car while I was small to get a closer look at the engine, but I didn't have time to ring the water out of my shirt, let alone monkey around with *The Bolt*'s performance. The race was starting in four minutes and twenty seconds, and it would take us three minutes and forty seconds to get there. Especially with Lin's skateboard being microsized.

"We'll have to come back and unshrink everything later," Lin said as I examined our last upgrade.

"Yeah. And we'll have to see if we can straighten out the Fruity Stars Lab, too. It's a shredded mess," I said.

I didn't have time to screw the Hammer of Doom to *The Bolt* like I had in the past, but I did the next best thing. I slipped my belt from my waist, circled it around the car, and tightened the upgrade to the top.

"Is that going to work?" Lin asked while she found an empty tin in my backpack that had once been full of mints.

"It might not smash down the same way it did before, but it's better than nothing," I said.

Lin pulled a fluffy piece of gauze from my first

aid kit and stuffed it in the box. She punched some holes in the top of the empty mint box with a nail she found on the floor of Penrod's barn-lab.

"How about this?" she asked.

"It's perfect," I said. I handed her the sleeping Pizza, and she put him and Cornelia in the box. Then she carefully tucked the new Microsaurus rex nursery in her pocket.

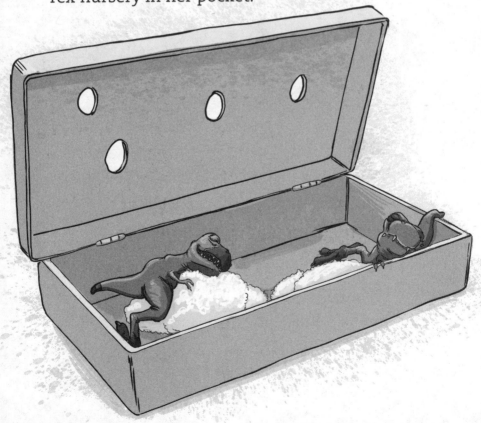

"I'm done," I said. "Let's RUN!"

Lin led me out of Professor Penrod's top secret barn, and I followed her as fast as I could as we made our way to the Dump Track.

It was 4:47 when we arrived, and Icky Vicky was ready to leave. Her driver was buzzing her purple bug around the track, and she was standing there with her arms crossed, tapping her foot, a bored look on her face.

"You're late, AND you're soaking wet," Icky Vicky said. "Classic Danny and Lin move."

"We had swimming lessons, too," I said as I swung my backpack off.

"Really? Were they in a mud puddle? Because you guys are filthy," Vicky said.

"You're just jealous. Everyone knows swimming in mud is good for your skin," Lin said.

"Not *that* kind of mud," Vicky said.

"We going to race or trade beauty secrets?" Lin asked.

I removed *The Bolt* from my backpack and started it up. I gave the controls to Lin and she spun it around in circles, kicking up a dust cloud so thick that Vicky coughed.

"Oh, we're going to race all right," Vicky said. "But where are all your upgrades?"

"We lost them in a desert while being chased by a pack of wild dinosaurs," I said, telling the truth since I knew there was no way she would believe it anyway.

"You guys are so weird," Vicky said.

"Weird and ready to win," Lin said.

"Daddy? Are you ready?" Vicky asked.

"Of course, Victoria, darling."

Lin parked *The Bolt* at the starting line, and Vicky's driver pulled the purple beetle up next to our RC car. While we'd been busy with an epic raptor battle, Vicky's car had been back in the shop. There were new upgrades hanging all over it, and most of them looked *very* familiar. It had a big speaker on the back, a glass

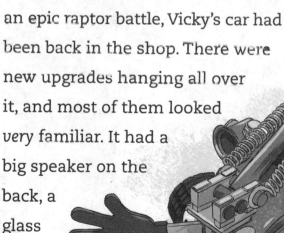

cannon filled with black goop, a grappling hook on a silver spool, and two big plastic hands that looked ready to slap. But the real kicker was the red hammer strapped to the top of the car.

"Boy, those upgrades look familiar," I said. "Wherever did you get the idea for those?"

Vicky looked over at me and wrinkled her nose, and right then I knew I wanted to beat her more than just about anything in the whole wide world.

"Are you ready?" Vicky's dad asked.

Lin was too focused to respond. I tapped Lin on the shoulder to get her attention. She looked ready to me, but I needed to know how she was feeling. "Are you ready for this?" I asked.

She looked at me and gave me a dangerous smile. "You kidding me? Dude. We just defeated a hungry pack of oviraptors while riding on the backs of Microsaurs. After that, beating Icky Vicky in an RC car race will be a walk in the park."

"Oh yeah. We're ready," I answered, full of confidence.

"On your mark! Get set! GO!!!" Vicky's dad shouted.

Both cars burst forward, sending dirt clods and goop spraying behind them in an arching rainbow. The cars were nose to nose going into the first turn.

"Smack them, Daddy!" Vicky shouted, and her dad pressed a button. The hands on top of the car took a swing at *The Bolt*, but Lin was ready for it. She swerved to the left, ducking under an old high chair.

"Fire the hammer, Danny," Lin said.

"Not yet," I said. The belt that I had tightened around *The Bolt* was starting to come loose, but it was still holding on to the Hammer of Doom. We'd have only one shot, so we had to make it count.

The Bolt raced around the course, but every time Lin made a move, the purple car was a second faster. "Blast them, Daddy. BLAST THEM!"

Vicky's dad pulled a trigger, and the speaker in the back of the purple beast boomed. The sound waves missed *The Bolt* by less than an inch, but they smashed the toilet bowl just behind the car into bits.

The race continued for two and a half laps. We were in the lead one second, then following the next. Lin was an RC-car-driving ninja, dodging every upgrade trick Vicky's car threw our way. We had half a lap left. Less than fifty yards stood between us and victory.

"It's hammer time, Danny," Lin said as we pulled up right behind the purple beetle.

"Not quite yet," I said. The Hammer of Doom was barely strapped to the roof of the car. It bounced and bobbled around with every bump in the road. The retaining arm, a metal rod at the base of the Hammer of Doom that kept it from launching forward like a missile, had fallen off somewhere during the race. I knew that the Hammer of Doom was going to go sailing as soon as I launched it, so I made up a new plan right there in the middle of the race. "Aim for the old diving board."

"But that's the wrong direction," Lin said.

"Trust me," I said. My finger hovered over the HoD button. I was ready to launch our one and only shot.

"I hope you're right, Danny," Lin said. She cranked the car to the left, and Vicky squealed with joy.

"Ha! You went the wrong way!" she said. "I'm going to win! I'm going to win!"

"Oh, no you're not," I whispered. Then, just as the front tires of *The Bolt* touched the diving board, I pressed the button.

The hammer swung so fast and hard it looked like a blur. Instead of crashing down on the ground in front of us, it launched forward, soaring through the air. It smashed into the glass screen of an old television. The TV toppled over, smashing down on the other end of the diving board. *The Bolt* was sent rocketing through the air. It flipped end over end, flying right over Icky Vicky's purple bug, and came down with a thud right in the middle of the finish line. Car parts sprang out from *The Bolt* in every direction. It was a total wreck, but we had won the race.

"NO! NOOOO! That did NOT just happen!"
Victoria Van-Varbles shouted.

Lin looked at me and gave me a wink. I held
out my fist to her and she gave it a little bump.

There was no need to brag, or rub our victory into Vicky's face. We'd won the race fair and square, had a fantastic adventure, and inside Lin's pocket were two sleeping, adorable twin Microsaurus rexes—our day had turned out pretty great!

"Hey, Vicky," Lin said. Vicky turned and glared at us. "Nice race."

"It was NOT a nice race, but I'm going to beat you next week, or my name isn't Victoria Van-Varbles," Vicky said.

Lin and I shared a glance and I knew exactly what she was thinking, and I felt exactly the same. I turned back to Vicky and smiled. "Actually, I think we're retiring from RC racing. *The Bolt* has run its last race."

"That's not fair!" Vicky said. "I want a rematch."

"Sorry, Vicky. But Danny's right. We're retiring from the racing circuit," Lin said.

"We'd stay and chat, but there's a Pizza that needs my attention," I said as I smiled at Lin.

We laughed as I stuffed what remained of *The Bolt* in my pack, then I walked side by side with my best friend toward home, knowing that the day had been pretty great indeed.

A VIDEO NOTE FROM PROFESSOR PENROD

"Hello again, Danny and Lin. I hope this goes through. Our last call was cut short. I tried to call you right back, but as I told you, the satellite phone here is a bit unpredictable.

"I thought that sending a message might be a little easier. By now you've taken care of the new Microsaurs in the package I sent. I'm sure they were quite a surprise, and I can't wait to find out what was inside the egg! I hope it hatched and is bouncing around happily in the Microterium.

"I'm also sending this to tell you that I've found something else very exciting. It will be the largest Microsaur in the collection. By far, I'd guess. I've been tracking the large Microsaurs for weeks now, and I think I'm getting very close. The area they live in is in danger of being destroyed to make room for a factory, so it's very important that I find them soon and bring them back to the safe and loving sanctuary of the Microterium before it's too late.

"I know you'll keep the old place in tip-top shape, and you should know that I'm forever grateful. So grateful in fact, that I'll be scheduling a trip home to say hello and pack a few new supplies for another trip! There are Microsaurs all over the planet that need our attention!

"Anyhoo. Best of luck with the new arrivals, and I'll see you soon!

"Oh, and remember. Adventure awaits!"

FACTS ABOUT OVIRAPTORS

- The name oviraptor really does mean "egg thief."
  The very first oviraptor fossils were discovered
  in China in 1924, by a paleontologist named
  Henry Fairfield Osborn. Osborn named the
  dinosaurs himself—which is one of the great
  things about discovering a dinosaur, by the way—
  but even he wasn't sure that the name was quite
  right.

- When Osborn discovered the oviraptor skeleton,
  lying beside it were some fossilized eggs. He
  could tell by the size of the eggs that they did
  not belong to the oviraptors, so he theorized

that the oviraptors had stolen the eggs so they could eat them. But as we learn in this book from Danny, a theory is just a guess, an idea filled with wonder, until it is proven. For decades scientists have studied the fossil records of the oviraptors, and they are still busy coming up with more fascinating theories about them every day.

- While the tiny-raptors in this book have grinning mouths that Lin describes as toothy, we know by the fossil records of actual oviraptors that they didn't have teeth at all. However, in place of teeth, the oviraptors had spikes that hung from the roof of their mouths. Creepy!

- Although a complete oviraptor skull has yet to be found, we have a pretty good idea of what it looked like because paleontologists are excellent puzzle solvers, and they have found the fossils of dinosaurs closely related to the oviraptors to compare against.

- It's fun to imagine what an oviraptor actually looked like, but if you want a pretty good living example, check out a bird from New Guinea called a cassowary. They are big, flightless birds with scaly, clawed, three-toed feet and a bony crest on their heads. Some people today even call them living dinosaurs, and they aren't far off. Fossil records show us that birds are the most likely descendants of dinosaurs, and while most drawings you see today of dinosaurs look more like lizards than chickens, we know for sure that a great deal of them were actually covered in feathers—you know, like a cassowary.

- Did oviraptors really growl and click? Well, we know they didn't sing like birds of today. Birds create their songs with an organ called a syrinx, which allows them to whistle, tweet, and sing, but oviraptors did not have this song-making device. They lived in dense rain forest and had to communicate across long distances, so paleontologists think they made low-pitched growls and clicks, because those sounds travel better over long distances. Once again, take a listen to a cassowary if you're interested in hearing a living example. They might be the closest thing we'll ever hear to an oviraptor.

- Oviraptors were probably really good parents. We know this because the most complete fossil record of the oviraptors found so far included a female oviraptor covering a nest of eggs. The fossil record tells us a lot about how she lived and how she died. A great sandstorm buried her alive, but even with the dangerous weather rushing all around her, this mother stayed with her nest no matter what.

- Oviraptors came in all sizes. Some were as small as the common chicken we have today, but the Gigantoraptor was way too big to fit in a chicken coop. While most oviraptors were less than five feet long, this massive creature could grow to twenty-six feet in length and weigh more than a ton!

ACKNOWLEDGMENTS

Here we are, at the end of the book, and I still haven't thanked those who helped me get here. Well, it's like they say. The last is the best of all the gang. So, here it is. A small and incomplete list of those who breathed life into the pages of this book.

Jodi, my partner in all things good.

Annie, who still thinks I'm funny even though she's a teenager.

Malorie, who will soon be faced with the hardest question a creative can have in life: which talent to feed. Thanks for inspiring me to choose mine.

Davis, who has been smarter than his old dad since he was nine years old, and not afraid to show it.

Tanner, who understands the value of hard work, which usually means he's too busy creating his art to help me with mine. A dad couldn't ask for more.

Gemma Cooper, who challenges and champions my crazy ideas.

Holly West, who kindly suggests a better path without bruising my fragile artist's ego.

Liz Dresner, who somehow pulls order out of thin air and adds design to my jumbled scratches.

The team at Feiwel & Friends for their continued support and encouragement.

And if you are still reading, well then, for crying out loud, I must acknowledge you, dear reader! The Page Turners. Without you, words go unread. Illustrations go unseen. And most important, wild stories go untold.

DUSTIN HANSEN, author of *Game On!* and the Microsaurs series, was raised in rural Utah. After studying art at Snow College, he began working in the video game industry, where he has been following his passions of art and writing for more than twenty years. Dustin can often be found hiking with his family in the same canyons he grew up in, with a sketchbook in his pocket and a well-stocked backpack over his shoulders.

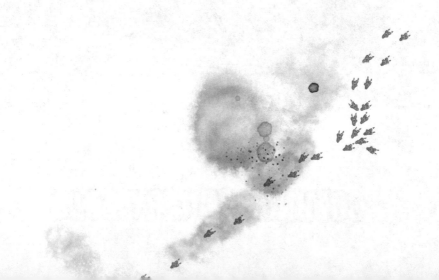

COMING JANUARY 2018

MICROSAURS

THAT'S MY TINY-SAURUS REX

Thank you for reading this **FEIWEL AND FRIENDS** book.

The friends who made

MICROSAURS

FOLLOW THAT TINY-DACTYL

possible are:

JEAN FEIWEL, Publisher
LIZ SZABLA, Editor in Chief
RICH DEAS, Senior Creative Director
HOLLY WEST, Editor
ELIZABETH BAER, Production Editor
RAYMOND ERNESTO COLÓN, Senior Production Manager
EMILY SETTLE, Administrative Assistant

Follow us on Facebook or visit us online at mackids.com.
OUR BOOKS ARE FRIENDS FOR LIFE.

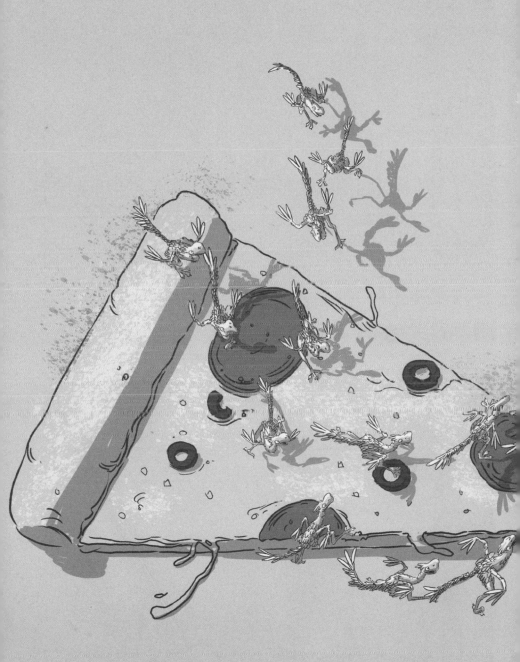